BAD BLOOD

Police detective Doug Orlando had a few things going against him as he hunted the killer of the radically righteous rabbi.

Blacks didn't trust him because he was white. Jews didn't trust him because he was a goy. Liberals didn't trust him because he was a cop. Fellow cops didn't trust him because he was gay. His partner was a cop who liked to shoot to kill and who hated him as a snitch. And one of his suspects, Leonard Lynch the real estate mogul, had a king-sized ego, a direct line to the mayor, and the clout to squash Orlando like a bug.

Against this, all that Orlando had was his smarts, his guts—and his job to do. . . .

FINAL ATONEMENT

Steve Johnson

A DOUG ORLANDO MYSTERY

AN ONYX BOOK

For the Bear
and for Patrick Dixon Fuller

ONYX
Published by the Penguin Group
Penguin Books USA Inc., 375 Hudson Street,
New York, New York 10014, U.S.A.
Penguin Books Ltd, 27 Wrights Lane,
London W8 5TZ, England
Penguin Books Australia Ltd, Ringwood,
Victoria, Australia
Penguin Books Canada Ltd, 10 Alcorn Avenue,
Toronto, Ontario, Canada M4V 3B2
Penguin Books (N.Z.) Ltd, 182–190 Wairau Road,
Auckland 10, New Zealand

Penguin Books Ltd, Registered Offices:
Harmondsworth, Middlesex, England

First published by Onyx, an imprint of New American Library,
a division of Penguin Books USA Inc.

First Printing, December, 1992
10 9 8 7 6 5 4 3 2 1

PUBLISHER'S NOTE
This is a work of fiction. Names, characters, places, and incidents either
are the product of the author's imagination or are used fictitiously, and
any resemblance to actual persons, living or dead, events, or locales is
entirely coincidental.

CHAPTER 1

The bedroom was stuffy with death.

Detective Doug Orlando stood silently over the body heaped on the floor. His brown eyes, set hard in a square-cut face, scrutinized the room. The lamp on the bedside table cast pale light over the corpse of a man sprawled on his back, arms loosely at his sides. Crushed under a close-cropped head sprouting curled locks of hair at each temple was a black fedora. A deep gash snaked its way from one ear to the other across his throat. Blood had spattered the dark trousers and jacket, and turned the white shirt bright red. A black and white prayer shawl, now blemished with blood, was stuffed into the victim's mouth. Glints of light caught on a blood-encrusted straight razor on the floor. A thick pool of crimson, too much to be absorbed by the rug, surrounded the body.

But that wasn't what caught Orlando's attention.

The rabbi's beard had been shaved off, roughly. Abrasions on his sickly white skin appeared through coarse stubble and tufts of hair missed by the razor.

The room was a mess. Drawers pulled, contents scattered. A wooden chair overturned. The broken pieces of a small lamp lay shattered at the feet of the dead man. Orlando focused on an ornate wooden shaving kit sitting open among toiletries on the bureau, the razor absent. Only the curtains drawn against the night, and the two double beds, their quilts neat and tucked in, were spared the rampage.

Orlando tightened his jaw, unbuttoned his overcoat, and went to work. Crouching over the corpse, he gently lifted a sallow wrist. Not yet cold. And rigor mortis hadn't set in. The medical examiner would determine exact time of death.

Orlando had been lucky tonight. Other than the beat cops called to the scene, he was the first of the investigative team to arrive, before forensics, the Crime Scene Unit photographer, and others had pawed the body and mauled the room. Being alone with the corpse was an almost spiritual experience for him, and sometimes his strongest hunches about the who and the why of the murder came to him in these moments.

But he didn't feel lucky. He just felt weary. People asked him if he ever got used to his job as a Brooklyn homicide cop. He looked down at the glassy eyes staring at the ceiling. No, he never got used to it.

"Pretty, huh?" a voice boomed from behind

him. "Well, whoever did it sure did a good job."

Orlando dropped the wrist and spun around. Detective Briggs stood framed in the doorway. Orlando's lip twisted in disgust. He was glad the widow was in the living room, out of hearing range. Allowing Briggs near the dead was blasphemous.

"What are you doing here?" Orlando growled.

Briggs's heavy black eyebrows rose innocently. "Me? Reilly assigned me. You and me will be working together again. Just like old times." He showed his teeth—big teeth, too big even for his wide mouth and fleshy lips—but it wasn't a smile.

Orlando scowled. "Reilly? Figures. We'll see about that later. In the meantime, just stay out of my way."

Briggs casually scratched short wavy hair flecked with gray, but his eyes shone meanly. "Buddy, it's you that better watch out. You're looking more and more like dead meat to me every day."

There was a scuffle of feet down the hall, and Briggs turned and grunted, "The gang's all here." He stepped into the room and the investigative team followed. They spread out, each doing his job. The CSU photographer shot pictures from each angle, shocks of white light bursting from his camera. The man from forensics, a stocky Hispanic who wore an oversized trench coat, a shaggy mustache, and a cocky air, began dusting the room for prints.

Brightman, the deputy medical examiner, stood by with his black leather bag enveloped by crossed arms and resting on his paunch until the photographer was done with the body, then moved in.

Their faces registered no expression, as if they saw the details of the murder but not the terrible death itself. Orlando hoped he would never become so hardened. If he ever did, he knew it would be time to leave the force.

Briggs went to check the back door, and Orlando searched the room. A checkbook and a bankbook lay on a bedside table, next to the telephone. He flipped through them. Nothing unusual. Shuffling through the ransacked clothes in the bureau drawers, Orlando found nothing that seemed out of the ordinary. He opened the closet door. It was only partially full, housing pressed black trousers and jackets, and white shirts.

"The guy was no Liberace, was he?" Briggs said from the doorway.

As if in answer, Orlando shut the closet door. "What did you find out back?"

"The door was open. It leads to an alley. Mrs. Rabowitz says it was always left locked. I'd say a pick and a torsion wrench were used. I'll have the tumblers checked for scratches to make sure."

Orlando watched Brightman bending over the body with scalpel in his rubber gloved hand, then looked away. The deputy medical examiner would make an incision at the rabbi's liver, plunge a thermometer in to establish time of death, then circle the slit with a yellow felt-tipped pen to differentiate this cut from the others on the body. Orlando didn't need to view the procedure—he'd seen it enough times in his ten years in homicide. He kneaded his chin with thick fingers and thought for a moment. "Where's the hair?" he said suddenly.

"Huh?" Briggs's eyes darkened as he stepped into the room.

"The hair," Orlando said. "He was shaved. Where's the hair?" There was no trace of hair around the body. He scanned under the beds. Only dust balls. Orlando motioned to the man from forensics. "Hernandez, come with me."

Orlando found the bathroom and flicked on the light switch. He studied the old-fashioned sink. There were a few bloody hairs, and drops of water around the drain were tainted pink with blood. Orlando stooped over the toilet and examined the inside of the bowl. "Well, they didn't flush the hair down the toilet. There would have been traces around the sides." Snapping back the shower curtain revealed nothing but a porcelain tub and checkered tiles. He jerked his head toward the sink. "Take samples of the hairs." Hernandez threw Orlando a cool look, but did as he was told.

Orlando made a quick search of the house. The hall opened on several doorways. In the first, a kitchen, he rifled through the garbage pail. Nothing. He passed a second doorway

and did a double take. It was another kitchen—
two kitchens? This one didn't seem to be
used; it was clean as the kitchen in a realtor's
open house. He checked the wastebaskets in
two children's bedrooms. The hair was nowhere to be found.

Orlando discovered Hernandez in the dining
room taking a scraping of a blood splotch on
the light switch. Another man from forensics
was on his knees, examining a throw rug.

"I want you and your team to go over every
inch of this place looking for that hair," he
ordered, even though he doubted they would
find any.

Hernandez nodded, but said nothing. He
wasn't a bad guy, but he toed the company
line. Everyone else was short with Orlando, so
he was, too. Orlando wondered whether the
man from forensics even knew why the rest of
the force was at his throat.

"Why take the hair?" Orlando asked when
he returned to the bedroom. "For that matter,
why shave him at all?"

Briggs and the CSU photographer stared at
him in glum silence. Brightman leaned against
the wall with arms crossed.

"A cult killing?" Hernandez asked, coming
up from behind. "Sure has the look of it."

Orlando folded his arms. He would have to
let the question ride for a while. Turning to
the forensics expert, he said, "You find any
fingerprints?"

Hernandez shook his head. "None on the

razor." He caught a glance from Briggs, and his tone toward Orlando became more clipped. "Must have used gloves. Lots of prints around the rest of the place, but I think we'll find they are the family's."

"What about the time of death?" Orlando said. "Brightman?"

The deputy medical examiner jolted to attention. "Midnight. Or damn close to it."

"Anything stolen?"

Briggs cleared his throat irritably. He liked to be the one asking questions. "Not according to Mrs. Rabowitz."

Orlando nodded and bit his lip. "Skinheads would have left a calling card—swastikas on the walls, something."

"I'm not sure why he was shaved," Briggs said. "It may have been just to knock us off track. Rabowitz comes home and walks straight into a burglary in progress. He wrestles with the intruder. The burglar panics and hits him on the head with the lamp, and then grabs the razor from the bureau he has been ransacking and gives the rabbi a good one right across the neck. Then ... who knows, he goes a little crazy and cuts the guy's beard off to confuse us ..."

Orlando bent over the body and pulled back the sheet Brightman had laid down after finishing his examination. The sheet was wet with crimson. The corpse had been moved from its original position onto its side. Orlando took a wallet from the back pocket; a wad of bills was stuffed inside. He studied the dead man with great care, slipped the wallet back in the pocket, then placed the sheet back and sighed. The scent was already cold. Too many clumsy hands obliterating clues. He looked up at Briggs. "And painstakingly picks up every trace of hair and takes it with him, and doesn't even bother to grab the wallet? And then stuffs a prayer shawl down the rabbi's throat? No way. Your theory's shit, Briggs."

"Maybe he panicked and ran. I've seen stranger things," Briggs said stiffly.

Orlando rose and shook his head. "No, Rabowitz was shaved before he ever came into the bedroom. The blood splotch in the dining room tells me that. After he was shaved, the rabbi probably put his hand to his bloody jaw, then touched the light switch in the dining room on his way to wash his face in the bathroom."

Brightman nodded. Briggs didn't move. He wouldn't give Orlando the satisfaction.

"The question is," Orlando continued, "where was he shaved? Not here in the apartment. There would have been hair somewhere."

"One thing's for sure," Briggs said. "He was killed in this room. The pool of blood proves that."

The doorbell rang and Orlando excused himself. It was probably just the assistant district attorney, but he wanted a chance to interview the widow alone. He had seen Briggs's tough tactics backfire and break down too

many good witnesses into incoherent jab-
bering. That might be fine for hardened crimi-
nals, but not for the families of victims. And
this killing didn't have the modus operandi of
a domestic quarrel gone fatal. He passed a
fresh-faced A.D.A. in the dining room, and
they exchanged friendly nods—the folks at the
D.A.'s office had nothing against him.

Mrs. Rabowitz braced herself behind a wooden
chair in the living room, her trembling hands
stroking its knobs and curves. Dark eyes, ac-
cented by even darker circles beneath them,
caught haunted shadows from the pole lamp
in the corner. She was a small woman, not
quite the height of Orlando's shoulder, and
she must have been in her thirties, but a total
absence of youthful resilience made pinpointing her exact age difficult.

Orlando knew the look in her eyes, recognized the stoop of her shoulders. He would
have to go easy; this woman was ready to col-
lapse. He stood in the arched doorway, taking
in the room. The air had a heaviness, a
stillness, as if it hadn't been disturbed by
laughter in years. The curtains were drawn,
appropriate for the late hour, but Orlando had
an inkling this home was always bathed in
shadow. The walls were lined with dimly illuminated bookshelves. Each piece of furniture
was an antique, solid and thick, adding to the
ponderous mood of the room. An open rolltop
desk, piled high with papers, occupied the
wall by the front door. A Persian rug, the color

of dried blood, cushioned his feet. He wondered at the kind of life this woman must live.

"Sorry to disturb you, Mrs. Rabowitz. I know how hard this must be for you. I'd like to ask you some questions, if I may." This was the part of his job he hated most: pressing the victim's family for painful details of the crime just when they were at their weakest. Sometimes these interrogations brought forth confessions, but usually they were just one added assault on people already reeling with sorrow.

She nodded and eased herself into the chair, as a woman twice her age would do. Her hair was auburn and cut very short, the features of her face, save her eyes, nondescript. But her eyes, they carried the weight of a burden Orlando couldn't fathom. A flowered scarf tied around her neck matched her dress.

Orlando crossed the room to a bookcase. Aged and obscure volumes crammed the shelves; most titles were in Hebrew. He pulled a pen and pad from his coat pocket.

"Can you tell me the last time you saw your husband alive?"

Her tiny hand went to her throat, and Mrs. Rabowitz let out a muffled sob. Then her face tightened and she quickly recovered, but her voice was a frayed thread strained to the breaking point. "It was this evening, dinnertime. We had a late dinner at seven-thirty. Avraham was in a bit of a hurry, what with his meeting and all."

"Meeting?"

"Yes. He and several of the other men from our synagogue have been getting together regularly. They talk politics, plan political strategies, study the Talmud."

Orlando made a note to find out if Rabowitz had ever made it to that meeting.

"He left home, oh, about eight-thirty, I would say."

"And that was the last time you saw him alive." Orlando hated himself the moment the words came out. It was so easy to twist the knife in the wound.

But Mrs. Rabowitz didn't flinch. "Yes."

Orlando walked to the mantelpiece. Silver candlesticks flanked the portrait of an ancient rabbi with piercing, kind eyes. A string of silver-framed photographs of children wound their way around the candlesticks and across the mantel. A little boy with a shaved head and yarmulke grinned with eyes shining. A girl with hair the color of her mother's, but blessed with soft curls, showed two big front teeth in an engaging smile. There were a couple of shots of a younger Mrs. Rabowitz cradling a baby in her arms, and one of a child of about three, staring inquisitively. These pictures were the only life in the room.

"After Avraham left, I took the kids to visit my sister and her family. They live just over in Brooklyn Heights." She paused. The further she continued telling the story, the more difficult it seemed to become.

"And what time did you leave your sister's?" Orlando gently prodded.

"About twelve-fifteen, I think. I got home just before twelve-thirty."

"Yes, your call to the police was logged at twelve twenty-nine." Orlando indicated the photographs. "How many kids do you have?"

"Three. Two boys and a girl."

Orlando glanced into the dining room and down the hallway studded with bedroom doors beyond. "You sent them to stay with neighbors?"

"Oh, no. They didn't come home with me. They stayed at my sister's. We adults—my sister Anna, her husband, and me—were up so late talking, the kids fell asleep in the playroom. I didn't have the heart to drag them out into the cold night—Rachel has the sniffles—so we put them to bed with Anna's children. They sleep over with one another a lot, though usually not on a school night."

"Under the circumstances, I think you're pretty lucky it turned out that way."

She shuddered.

"So you arrived home a few minutes before twelve-thirty."

Mrs. Rabowitz nodded. "When I first stepped in the door, I felt something was wrong. The light in the dining room was on, as I had left it. We always leave a light on to fool burglars when we're not home. But there was something . . . different."

"Something different?"

"At first I couldn't tell what it was, then I saw that the lamp in our bedroom down the hall was on. I was sure I had turned it off before I left. I thought maybe Avraham had returned home from the meeting, but it was so quiet. I called out to him. There wasn't a sound. When I walked into the dining room . . ." She indicated the archway leading into the formal dining room furnished in heavy oak with a long china cabinet housing delicate dishes. ". . . I saw that . . . mark."

Orlando's eyes zeroed in on the dark red spot on the light switch that Hernandez had taken scrapings of earlier.

"Then I really panicked. I wanted to run and hide. I was terrified. I called Avraham's name. There was no answer. I knew he might be in trouble, and I had to be brave. I crept down the hall and into our bedroom." Her voice quavered, and she covered her face with hands as white and fine as the china in the dining room cabinet. Mrs. Rabowitz's muffled voice burst forth through suppressing hands: "And Avraham was on the floor. Dead."

Orlando took a Kleenex from a box on the rolltop desk and handed it to her. She wiped her nose and held the crumpled tissue in a small fist in her lap.

"Then I called the police."

"You didn't call an ambulance first?" Orlando spoke gently. It was not an accusation.

The widow blinked. "You saw him. I knelt down over Avraham. He wasn't breathing.

There was no pulse. There was no doubt in my mind that he was dead."

For the first time, Orlando saw a black stain on her dress.

Mrs. Rabowitz caught his gaze, and her face seemed to crumble in pain. "When I bent down on my knees, I got blood on my dress. I thought of changing it, but then I thought the police might not like me doing that."

Orlando nodded. "I'm sorry, Mrs. Rabowitz. If you'd like to change now . . ."

She shook her head quickly. "I just want to see my children. Can I call my brother-in-law to come pick me up? I don't think I can drive."

Orlando glanced at the phone. A gray powder had been sprinkled on it—the forensics team had already dusted for prints. "Sure. Just one more question. Can you think of anyone who would want to kill your husband?"

Mrs. Rabowitz thought for a long moment. She began to speak, seemed to think better of it, then looked at him with frightened eyes. She whispered, "I don't know."

"Think about it. We'll talk more later." He slipped his notepad in his pocket. "Why don't you call your brother-in-law now? We'll take care of everything."

She nodded gratefully, and with an unsteady hand began to dial the phone on the table.

Pulling open the front door, Orlando found a uniformed officer standing guard. Behind him, Mrs. Rabowitz spoke into the telephone. "It's me, Michael, Sarah." Her voice broke. She sobbed into the mouthpiece that her husband had been murdered.

Orlando stepped through the door and out of earshot. After all this time, it was still tough to hear. Years ago, his own father had been murdered. His mother still mourned. He remembered the pain. Mrs. Rabowitz would have her anniversaries of sadness, too.

"Are our men canvassing?" Orlando asked.

The officer's words showed respect, but not his intonation. "Yes, sir. We're interviewing all the neighbors. So far, nobody saw nothing. We got men out back in the alley looking around."

Orlando glanced down the tree-lined street of well-maintained brownstones, so typical of Brooklyn. But he knew this neighborhood, Williamsburg, was different from the others. Men in hastily thrown-on clothes clustered on the sidewalk across the street, yarmulkes on their heads. They'd been awakened by a knock on the door from New York's finest, and grilled on what they'd seen. And Orlando could feel other neighbors peering out their darkened windows. That was good. Someone must have seen something earlier. He couldn't hear what the men across the way were saying, until one spoke heatedly above the rest. "This never would have happened if we'd done like the rabbi said. We should have started the patrols a long time ago. You can't even walk in this neighborhood anymore without being accosted by some nigger."

Orlando shook his head. Things could get ugly if he didn't find the killer soon.

A few minutes later, a red Mercedes pulled to the curb, and a man in a loose green turtleneck with a black leather bag in hand slipped from behind the wheel. He was big; his large buttocks and swelling stomach made him resemble a giant pear. The man's clothes told Orlando that he was not a Hasid, not even Orthodox—there was no yarmulke on his head. Lumbering up the stairs, he offered Orlando a beefy paw.

"I'm Dr. Greenberg, Sarah's brother-in-law."

Orlando introduced himself and let Greenberg inside. Mrs. Rabowitz sat stiffly in the same chair, her hands gripping the armrests, knuckles white. When she saw the men, she burst into tears. "Oh, Michael," she cried.

"Everything is going to be all right, Sarah," Greenberg said. He set the bag on the table and rummaged inside, withdrawing a syringe. "If you've finished questioning her, I'd like to give Sarah something to calm her down."

Orlando nodded.

Greenberg prepared the syringe, then swabbed her arm with a cotton ball. Orlando smelled rubbing alcohol. When the job was done, the doctor recapped the needle and set it back in the black bag along with a vial of medicine. Orlando couldn't read its label. Greenberg asked to speak with him privately.

In the dining room, Greenberg spoke in the low tones Orlando supposed he used when telling relatives of medical realities he didn't want his patients to hear. "I want to ask a favor of you," he said. His eyes were gray and troubled. His face, too, was pear-shaped, with wide jaws and fat cheeks. A soft peach fuzz capped his bald head. "Avraham was not on speaking terms with his brother. I would appreciate it if you would inform him of the rabbi's death. They had a falling out some time ago." He glanced at Mrs. Rabowitz, who sat staring blankly at the photographs on the fireplace mantel. "I don't think Sarah is going to be in any shape to let him know, and frankly, I think she's afraid of him. I would do it but, well, there are certain things I would just as well not be involved in." He gave Orlando a look that said going to see Avraham Rabowitz's brother would explain what he meant. He told Orlando the brother's name and address.

Orlando asked him what time Mrs. Rabowitz left his house that evening.

"Around twelve-fifteen," he said. He corroborated the rest of her story, then asked if he could take her to his place. Orlando walked them to the door.

After they left, the stacks of papers on the rolltop desk caught his eye. He rifled through them haphazardly. Bills, mortgage payments, checks from tenants in apartment buildings the rabbi obviously owned. There were seller's

copies of receipts and an uncashed check from
an antique shop on Seventy-second and Madison in Manhattan. Serrout Antiques. But no
description of the objects of the transaction.
Orlando wondered what Rabowitz was selling
to an antique shop. The receipts were for a lot
of money. He set them aside and continued.
At the bottom of the pile were several dozen
option agreements, all for buildings in Williamsburg. It looked like Rabowitz was trying
to buy up whole blocks. The total price for
the property would be staggering. Hundreds of
millions of dollars. Why had the dead man
been optioning all these buildings, and where
would he get that kind of money to buy them?

The medical examiner's men arrived with a
stretcher, and Orlando led them to the bedroom. The pool of blood had been cleaned up
and samples taken, but the rug was still damp
and held a rust discoloration. The attendants
heaved the rabbi onto the stretcher, leaving
only a tape outline of where the body had
fallen. The straight razor had been bagged and
lay inside a leather case where Hernandez de-
posited other evidence of the crime—the blood
scrapings from the dining room, the hair from
the sink, the wooden shaving kit.

The investigative team followed the attendants carrying the body out of the room. Orlando locked the front door as they left the
brownstone—Mrs. Rabowitz had provided an
extra set of keys. Most of the neighbors standing across the street had drifted back to their

homes. Only a few lingered, whispering among themselves. Orlando buttoned his overcoat to the coldness of the night, and watched the stretcher being lifted into the ambulance. At the foot of the stairs, Briggs spoke quietly with the uniform standing guard.

When Orlando joined them, Briggs grunted, "Our men didn't find anything in the alley. And none of the neighbors saw a thing. Not one witness. I find that hard to swallow."

"It's late," Orlando shrugged. "This is a quiet neighborhood. People go to bed early."

"Yeah." Briggs grinned. "Early to bed, early to rise, makes a Jew wealthy ... wealthy ... *wealthy*." The uniform chuckled.

Orlando cast Briggs a stony look. "They don't look so wealthy here to me." He pulled his pad from his coat and flipped through his notes. He had all he was going to get tonight. What he needed now was the medical examiner's report. He hoped Ronnie Bell would perform the autopsy. "I'm taking off. I'll file my report in the morning. And I'm going to have a little chat with Lieutenant Reilly about partnering us up."

"You do that, pal. But you of all people ought to know what happens to guys who rock the boat." Briggs stepped to his Plymouth at the curb, pulled open the door, then looked back at Orlando. With a jerk of his head, he indicated Orlando's Chevy across the street in the shadows. "A cop ought to know better than to park his car in a dark area." Eyes gleaming, he smiled in the ungiving manner of a television preacher. "A guy could get his car vandalized that way."

CHAPTER 2

As Orlando crossed the street, a sickening sense of foreboding knotted his stomach. What stunt had they pulled this time? They were like mischievous schoolboys, but with a deadly difference. He felt the eyes of the other cops on the street etch into his back, waiting for his reaction. Whatever they had done, he wasn't going to give them the satisfaction of showing his anger. That only goaded them further.

Then he saw it: the word "FAGGOT" scratched in scrawly letters across the door of his blue Chevy. He clenched his teeth and keyed the lock. Briggs chuckled loudly from across the street. Without looking back at them, Orlando pulled open the door and slid inside. His face burned with rage as he revved the engine, slammed the car in gear, and sped down the street. He would get back at them, but in his own way, in his own time. For now, he would have to swallow his pride and put up with it. But in the end, he would outlast Briggs, and he'd outlast the rest of them. They could make him miserable, but they couldn't make him resign.

Orlando stared blindly ahead as one neighborhood melted into another, and wondered how it had ever come to this. After nearly twenty years on the force, this was his reward. All those years of seeing faces come and go, sharing the fears on the beat, mourning with the widows of cops shot down in the line of duty, watching buddies descend into the bottle or worse. Careers built, careers destroyed. And this was what it had come to. He didn't have a friend on the force. There wasn't a man in the Brooklyn P.D. who could stand him. It was like an agonizing divorce. As painful as a death in the family. And all because of his damned testimony for a cause already lost in a case forgotten by the public as quickly as the headline of yesterday's tabloid.

All because of a retarded black kid with an arrest record as long as your arm and a future about as bright as the Black Hole of Calcutta. A kid nobody cared about except maybe his mother, and even that was a big maybe.

It was just a fluke that it happened at all, but Orlando discovered it was those crazy little twists of fate that left you the bitterest after they'd done their dirty work. Homicide cops usually work alone in New York City, so it was just by accident that he and Briggs were together running down a lead on a murder case a year and a half earlier. It was a sweltering day in July. Heat rose from the pavement like suppressed anger, and their shirts stuck to their backs. Briggs, as usual, was in a bad mood. The radio squawked a burglary in progress, the perpetrator a black kid in a white neighborhood. A "regular." It was a job for the uniform cops, but the detectives were just blocks from the scene, and Briggs spun the car around and Orlando flipped on a screaming siren and clamped a pulsing light to the roof.

They saw the kid immediately. Running from the house with something black in his hand.

Briggs jammed on the brakes and was out of the car, gun in hand, yelling for him to stop.

The youth kept running.

Don't, Orlando's mind screamed as he jumped out of the car and crouched in firing position. *Not with Briggs. You don't play games with Briggs, kid!* Not when he has a gun aimed at your back.

Briggs yelled a second time. The punk made for a wooden fence.

Briggs downed the kid when he tried to scale the fence, his Smith & Wesson reporting like a crack of lightning. Orlando stared as the boy clung to the fence like an animal wounded but still fighting for life. Then Briggs shot him again, and the youth crumbled on the ground in a bloody heap.

And that would have been the end of it.

The shooting was justifiable under common police procedure. A burglary suspect, dark threatening object in fist, refusing to halt under police order. Briggs claimed the object looked like a gun. It had all happened so fast. When Briggs prodded the body after the shooting, the object turned out to be a narrow case for a costume jewelry necklace.

And that would have been the end of it. *Except*. Except Orlando couldn't forget the wounded youth clinging helplessly on a fence, and the second bullet trouncing an already crippled form into a lifeless heap. The image invaded his sleep, marred his waking hours.

There were immediate calls from black activists like the Reverend Melvin Packard for Briggs's prosecution, but they didn't have much of a case. The legal system doesn't come down too hard on white cops who shoot black punks with a record a mile long.

No one on the force thought twice about the case, least of all Briggs. Until Doug Orlando stepped forward to testify against him.

For years, Orlando hadn't liked Briggs. He knew what Briggs was, and anyone who knew what Briggs was didn't like him. But the two men went back a long way, to Orlando's first days as a rookie assigned to the more experienced Briggs. Briggs taught him all he knew, how to survive. How to deal with a domestic dispute without getting your head blown off. How to position yourself during an armed robbery. The lessons he had learned at the academy didn't mean much on the street, and Briggs showed him how to thrive on the beat. And Briggs had what every cop wants: respect from law-abiding citizens and fear from everyone else.

But Orlando's esteem for his partner withered.

Spending eight hours a day in the confines of a squad car revealed the real Briggs. The meanness of spirit edged with cruelty. The selective enforcement of the law to harass whomever he didn't like—especially minorities. The handcuffs so tight they cut off circulation. That relished, unnecessary jab with the nightstick.

That wasn't the kind of cop Orlando wanted to be. After being partners for a year, Orlando asked to be reassigned. He never said why, and afterward his relations with Briggs had been cool.

Orlando's fellow officers thought his testimony came easily, but it was the hardest thing he had ever done. There were so many reasons against sticking his neck out. Briggs would never be convicted, and it was absurd to think otherwise. Orlando couldn't remember when a cop had been convicted of killing a black kid. The truth was, Orlando might lose everything he had worked for.

But he kept thinking about that unnecessary second bullet. He couldn't get it out of his mind. And if Orlando didn't make a stand against his former partner, hadn't he become just another Briggs?

When the grand jury probe found no wrongdoing on Briggs's part, everything changed. Friendships of twenty years ended without a

word. Even old partners whose lives Orlando
had saved—and who had saved his—would no
longer look him in the eye. Orlando's good
friend Bill Shaw, a black sergeant, had cut
him off with a blanket of silence. That had
been especially tough. Shaw was respected by
all the men—Orlando included—and his rejec-
tion seemed to justify everyone else's.

It wasn't that the whole station house thought
Briggs had done the right thing. On the con-
trary, they knew he was a hothead. *But you
didn't snitch on other cops.* The code was the
code, something they had to live by, something
they couldn't survive without, and you just
didn't flout the code and expect ever to be a
viable part of the force again.

Even the few cops who were sympathetic
were afraid to be seen with him, and he didn't
press. Orlando knew he was poison, and those
who associated with him would find themselves in the same position that he was in. And
so a man who had been a loner on the force to
begin with became simply alone.

Orlando lived in Carroll Gardens in Brooklyn. It was a solid, old-fashioned Italian neighborhood swiftly being taken over by yuppies.
Old widows who stared silently out windows
and never learned a word of English, never
had to, were rapidly being replaced by young
professionals with shiny cheeks, Armani suits,
and Gucci briefcases. It was rumored that this
was Mafia territory, that thugs didn't dare

burglarize apartments or steal cars in this neighborhood. This myth may have stopped black and Hispanic punks from marauding in Carroll Gardens, but it didn't restrain the smart-ass Italian kids, who knew better.

Orlando swung down Sackett Street and wrestled the Chevy into a parking space between a BMW and a Mercedes. "Yuppies," Orlando grumbled, but half in jest. He didn't hold the resentment against the newest wave of immigrants into the area that many of the old-timers did, but wryly wondered when the corner pizza parlors would be replaced by Häagen-Dazs stands. And Orlando's mother—who owned several brownstones on the block, including the one he lived in—had certainly reaped the rewards of skyrocketing rents and real estate values brought by the now popular neighborhood.

Light bled through the curtains of the living room windows of his second-floor flat. Orlando remembered that it was exam week and let out a sigh. Four times a year, like the coming of the seasons, and just as predictable. The dishes didn't get washed, the laundry didn't get done, and Orlando didn't get any sex.

Orlando discovered his other half reclining in an easy chair in the living room, snoring. There was a half-graded exam in Stewart's lap, a felt-tipped pen dangling from the fingers of his right hand. His eyeglasses lay on an oak table next to the chair, along with a coffee mug stenciled with his name. Two stacks of papers towered from the carpet. The taller one, Orlando guessed, was yet to be graded.

Their dog, at the foot of the chair, stirred, his eyes mournful. Poindexter sniffed indifferently at an ashtray on the floor overflowing with cigarette butts, then settled back into a deep slumber. His floppy basset ears hung halfway over his eyes, forming blinders to the light, then spilled over onto the rug, creating carpets of their own. He let out a satisfied grunt.

Orlando looked away from the dog and grunted himself. "That's not how you get the exams graded."

Stewart snorted in his sleep, then woke with a start. "Huh?"

"Sleeping on the job. What are your students going to think?"

Stewart was an English professor at NYU. During exams week, he always burned the midnight oil—he said the kids deserved as much, since they had done the same when studying for them. These were the only weeks of the year that Stewart went back to smoking, but he did it with a vengeance. The pall of smoke covering the room could have killed a canary.

Stewart put on his glasses and focused on the clock above the carved-marble fireplace, then looked back at Orlando. "Jesus Christ," he said. "It's past three-thirty. They're working you around the clock deliberately. You've got to get out of that place."

Orlando didn't say anything. He didn't want to have this conversation again. Not now, not when he might just agree with everything Stewart said. He knew he'd have to tell his lover about the car, but not tonight. All he wanted at the moment was a cup of coffee and to drop into bed. He gave Stewart a quick kiss, hung his coat in the closet, and went into the kitchen.

Orlando's Italian mother had taught him family recipes during his childhood, and over the years he and Stewart had concocted some amazing Old Country dishes in this room. He breathed in the rich aroma of coffee brewing. If anything could revive his spirits, coffee would. Delicious Jewish pastries—Rugalach and Schnecken—nestled on a plate on the table. Stewart came from a Jewish family, but he was really second-generation atheist. The goodies he bought from the deli down the block and his insistence on bagels on Sunday morning were the most evident indication of his ancestry. Orlando found the mug with his name stenciled on it in the dish rack and poured himself a cup of decaf. Dishes were piled high in the sink. Exam week.

He settled in a chair, bit into a pastry, and glumly sipped the coffee. There was a time when he didn't mind the abrupt calls in the night ordering him to the murder scene—looked forward to them in fact—but that was before the grand jury investigation, before his testimony, before he was shunned by his fel-

low officers. Now the late-night calls were just
a harassment technique devised by Lieutenant
Reilly to drive him crazy. Since his testimony,
the most sordid murder cases in the borough
were dumped in his lap. Horrors that kept him
awake the nights the scream of the telephone
didn't.

Rising, he stepped to the cabinet above the
refrigerator and pulled down a bottle of rum.
This was against the rule he had set for himself long ago—a cop who takes a drink after
work may find one day that he can't stop.
Guiltily, he splashed a jigger in his mug then
plopped back in the chair.

Orlando studied his distorted image in the
shiny surface of the toaster on the table.
Crows feet were firmly planted at the corners
of his eyes. His nose, straight but slightly up-
turned, was met by a mustache so thick, it
looked like the bristles of a shoe brush and,
like his temples, was streaked with gray. He
raked his fingers through his hair, thinner
than it used to be, and receding. His hand
came to rest on a bald patch at the back of his
head. It wasn't so long ago, he didn't have *that*
problem. He shook his head. He looked too old
to be forty-two.

He knocked back the last drops of his drink.
It didn't taste as good as he hoped it would,
and it didn't do the trick. Nothing could revive the part of him that once had enthusiasm
for this job.

Wandering into the living room, Orlando

found Stewart absorbed in an exam. "You coming to bed?" Orlando said, leaning against a wall Stewart had painted off-white the month before. Stewart was always changing or improving something in the apartment: sanding and varnishing the parquet floors, buying a new print to hang, rearranging the furniture. Their building was the best Marie Orlando owned, a landmark really, with ornate moldings and high ceilings, and Stewart's artistic sense perfectly melded their modern furniture with the restored interior of the turn-of-the-century brownstone.

"Later."

With a sigh, Orlando turned and went down the hall to the bedroom. When had he ceased to be able to share his feelings with his lover? When had Stewart stopped listening? All he knew was that the issues most important to his life had become off-limits in their conversations. Orlando removed his holster and laid his Smith & Wesson on the bureau, shed his clothes and slipped into bed. But he didn't sleep. The neighbor's dog howled at the night, and Orlando's head swam with images of strange men in black fedoras who lived in a part of town that people like him never went to.

CHAPTER 3

The door to Reilly's office was open when Orlando arrived at the station house early Tuesday morning. The lieutenant's office was bigger than those of the homicide detectives, and had larger windows, but nothing could conceal the dismal institutional quality of the room. Metal desk, metal files. Venetian blinds gone yellow with age and smoke. A sickly plant in a plastic pot fought for light in the corner by the door. Reilly looked up from a stack of papers on his desk. Orlando had never seen him *do* anything with them, and assumed they were there for show: the overburdened watch lieutenant drowning in a sea of paperwork.

"You got a problem?" There was a puffiness to the lieutenant's face, a redness, that always reminded Orlando of an Easter Sunday ham. Reilly's sharp blue eyes were almost hidden behind thick white brows.

"Yeah, I got a problem that shoots little black boys in the back when I'm looking and vandalizes my car when I'm not." Orlando nudged some papers aside and set down a

Styrofoam coffee cup bought from the machine in the lounge. He began to take off his coat.

"Don't bother. You won't be here long." The lieutenant enunciated each word to press the double meaning. Reilly had had it in for Orlando since the grand jury investigation; the lieutenant wouldn't rest until he was booted from the force. Reilly didn't have much time—the old bastard would be retiring in a year, so he'd laid the pressure on thick in the last few months. But assigning Orlando to work with Briggs was his dirtiest trick.

Orlando pulled off his coat anyway, hung it over his forearm, and sat in a wooden chair in front of the desk. "I won't work with Briggs. You know that." He was surprised his voice came out a growl.

Reilly's canopy eyebrows rose innocently. "Yeah? And why not? He's a great cop. You just let him loose. He's ... like a goddamn bloodhound."

"Bullshit." More like a rabid junkyard dog, Orlando thought. "I won't do it."

"Oh, yes you will." Reilly's jowls wobbled as he nodded his head. "I'm *assigning* you. I need my two best men on this case." He paused slyly, then added. "Unfortunately, O'Roark retired last week, so I'm stuck with you." The lieutenant glowed with satisfaction. "Unless, of course, you want to transfer out of Homicide." There was a glint in his eye. "Or resign."

Orlando felt his fist clench around the coffee cup. *Don't let them make you angry, that's what they want to see.* "Fat chance. You'll be history in this place before I am."

Reilly shrugged. "We'll see." He pushed back from his desk and walked to the coffee maker in the corner. The department had provided Reilly with the coffee machine—one of the privileges of his position, and it was said that his coffee was superior to that in the lounge. Orlando didn't know—he'd never been offered any.

"About this murder," Reilly said. "I'm worried that things could get nasty. Real nasty. I've already asked the medical examiner's office to do the autopsy pronto." Reilly scratched his stomach absentmindedly. He had a large belly and balanced the extra weight by leaning backward, like a pregnant woman.

"And I don't want any sensationalism from the press," Reilly added. "We're keeping a lid on the more bizarre aspects of the case—don't mention the shaving or the missing hair to any reporters just yet. Wait till we find out what it all means. Otherwise the tabloids will be screaming about a mad rabbi shaver stalking the city."

Orlando shrugged. It wasn't unusual to withhold some details of a murder from the press. "Word will get out eventually anyway."

Reilly poured himself a cup and took a taste. "Man, that's good mud." Smiling thinly, he rounded his desk and took his seat. "You real-ize who Rabbi Avraham Rabowitz was, don't you?"

Orlando frowned. The name had struck him as familiar the night before, but he couldn't make a connection.

"I'd think you'd remember that name. After all, Rabowitz spent years campaigning against that, uh, Gay Rights Bill."

Orlando could tell Reilly thought he was doing him a big favor by using the word "gay." Orlando nodded. "Yes, I remember now." Rabowitz had been a controversial, though minor, figure on the New York political scene. He'd spent years campaigning against the Gay Rights Bill, bitterly condemning its passage in 1986. Orlando also vaguely remem-bered Rabowitz running for mayor on the Right-to-Life ticket. And there had been scrapes with blacks because of the condition of the apartment buildings he owned in Wil-liamsburg. Avraham Rabowitz had plenty of enemies in the city. Just knock on any door.

"Nasty case," Reilly muttered again, shak-ing his head. "In a lot of ways. And we could have problems in the community."

Orlando knew what he meant. He remem-bered the conversation of Rabowitz's neigh-bors that he overheard the night before. There were enough tensions between minority groups in Brooklyn without the dry kindling of a minority-motivated killing. Williamsburg was an enclave of Hasidic Jews and blacks, residing uneasily side by side. Though it was located only a handful of subway stops from the neighborhood where Orlando had spent his entire life, Williamsburg was foreign territory, unknown, peopled by denizens who viewed the world in ways he would never understand, with rituals and rites he could not fathom. The Hasidic men, with their long beards, curls at the temples, black fedoras, baggy black coats and trousers. The women, dressed modestly, heads covered with scarves, shopping at Hasidic stores with a string of children in tow, the boys with shaved heads and yarmulkes, buying foods Orlando had heard of but never tasted. And then there were the blacks, poorer, resentful of being squeezed out of the neighborhood by the more affluent Hasidim with their burgeoning families, whose ever increasing numbers ate away at the already limited amount of housing.

Reilly studied him. "Could've very easily been one of your buddies."

Orlando grimaced. So that was it. At last, the real reason he'd been awakened in the middle of the night and assigned to this case. It wasn't the murder. Any homicide detective could have handled it. It was the possible murderer. Reilly thought the killer might be homosexual, and he loved the idea of putting Orlando on a case that might be detrimental to the gay community. A case that would make Orlando miserable.

Reilly's eyes shone.

"I seriously doubt that, Lieutenant. But I'll take the case where the evidence leads me."

"Well, make sure it leads by Briggs's office, because you two will be sticking together from now on, like gum to a shoe."

Setting down his cup, Orlando rose and strode to the door. He had to get out before he throttled Reilly's fat neck.

"Hey, you!" Reilly growled, snatching up the empty Styrofoam cup. "You think I'm your maid? What am I supposed to do with this?"

Orlando turned back and began to speak, stopped, smiled to himself. "Sometimes, Reilly, you make it just too easy."

Orlando pushed the button with the down-pointing arrow and waited for the elevator doors to slide open. He wondered why morgues always seemed to be situated in the basement, or in this case, the subbasement. Perhaps it was comforting to some, as if this temporary holding place was a halfway house between the world of the living and final rest in the ground. More likely, its placement was a reflection of society's inclination to sweep the disturbing subject from sight, banishing it from view like a mad relative in a gothic horror tale.

The doors opened like an invitation to hell, and Orlando stepped inside and began his descent. When the elevator stopped in the basement, a fresh-faced attendant in surgical greens, who couldn't have been more than twenty, wheeled in a gurney carrying a form covered by a sheet. The attendant fixed his eyes on the numbers above the door as the elevator hummed into motion. Orlando watched the still form on the gurney out of the corner of his eye.

Despite all his years as a homicide cop, trips to the morgue never ceased to make Orlando uneasy. There was something fundamentally distressing in witnessing the dead in this impersonal setting. It was obscene, somehow, to take the remains of once vibrant people and place them on pans of stainless steel to be prodded, sliced, examined, and analyzed by those whose professionalism—whose very sanity—rested on the necessity to divorce the corpse lying before them from the living, loving being it had once been.

It took a special breed to perform this job, day after day. Orlando wasn't sure as a general rule how he felt about pathologists. He had a certain ambivalence toward those who chose this profession, but he supposed some might feel the same way about him. *Why had he become a homicide cop?*

One thing he knew: he liked Ronnie Bell, one of the medical examiners, very much. The feeling, apparently, was mutual. Ronnie was one of the few people involved in police work who stood by him since the grand jury investigation. She was in her early forties, and came from a generation of lesbians who didn't care who knew it. She had once told Orlando that

dressing the way she did freed her from sexual harassment by male coworkers, and made
a firm statement about femininity to boot.
Women were no longer going to allow men to
define female beauty. Of course, looking the
way she did brought snickers from some, but
her fuck-you-very-much attitude soon stopped
detractors cold. She was not the most popular
person in the medical examiner's office, but
she was treated with politeness and respect.
And for Ronnie, that was more important than
having their friendship.

When the subbasement didn't have the cop-
pery smell of blood, it reeked of formaldehyde.
The place seemed timeless. No windows to let
in the light of the early morning; only monotonous fluorescent lights droning from above.
The door to the examination room was open,
and Orlando stepped inside. Plenty of stainless steel and glossy paint—shiny, hard, ster-
ile, and mean; an affront to life. Ronnie sat in
a swivel chair, her back to the door, hunched
over a desk, elbows planted on the blotter,
chin resting in her fists. She was absorbed in
yesterday's *Post*. Orlando peered over her
shoulder. The tabloid's garish pages were
wrinkled with finger impressions as if it had
been read and reread. The headline screamed:
"BOMB BLASTS BROOKLYN ABORTIONIST."

Orlando knew the case. An abortion clinic
in Williamsburg had been bombed Monday
morning. One of the two women who ran the

clinic had her hand blown off in the explosion. So far, there had been no arrests.

Ronnie started when she realized she was not alone and slapped the newspaper shut. She swung around to face him.

"Oh!" she said. "It's you." Relief flooded cloudy eyes. Ronnie had the protruding front teeth of a cartoon rabbit. Her hair was sandy, with a boyish cut. Thick aviator-style glasses magnified pale blue eyes. Her white lab coat hung open. She wore a Star Trek T-shirt that suggested no breasts and blue levis faded at the knees. "I suppose you're here about the Rabowitz case."

Orlando pulled up a chair. "Yeah. What have you got for me?"

She pulled a folder from a drawer. "The report's right here."

"You didn't perform the autopsy?"

Ronnie was meticulous with details. Many crimes would never have been solved without her painstaking approach. She opened the folder. "No," Ronnie said. "That was done before I came on shift. I wouldn't have performed the autopsy without family permission, and as I see from the report, Hennessy didn't bother to contact the widow."

Orlando blinked. "We don't need permission in a murder case."

"That's beside the point. The guy was a Hasidic Jew."

"So?"

She shrugged. "Those people find the practice abhorrent. They believe the body should remain whole for the resurrection when the Messiah comes."

Orlando nodded in interest. The things he learned being a cop.

"Anyway, they should have at least asked the widow first as a courtesy. I don't much care for the politics of the Hasidim, but one thing you find out working down here is that we're all pretty much the same in the final analysis, and a little respect can go a long way to alleviate the family's pain. End of lecture."

Orlando cleared his throat. "You're sure fun and games today."

"Sorry, pal. I've got things on my mind." Her smile was thin.

Orlando changed his tone. He knew it was best not to push Ronnie. "Amy okay?" Her lover Sally had a child through artificial insemination several years ago.

"She's in kindergarten already, can you believe it?" Her eyes lighted at the thought, then dimmed just as quickly. Something was wrong, but Orlando could see she didn't want to talk about it. She became businesslike. "Now, let's see. Time of death." She flipped through the pages of the report. "We can place it pretty accurately at midnight."

Orlando nodded.

"Cause of death: suffocation."

Orlando frowned. "Wait a minute. It wasn't the razor slashing that killed him?"

Ronnie shook her head. "No. I'd say he was

incapacitated by getting his throat cut. The carotid was ripped. His heart literally pumped the blood out of his body. Must have been pretty messy."

Hard and fierce, Orlando pictured the murder scene again. The ashen face, the angry wound, the pool of crimson. "Pretty messy."

"I would guess he was near death from blood loss when the prayer shawl was stuffed down his throat."

"But he might have survived the throat cutting if he hadn't been smothered?"

She raised her hands as if the question was irrelevant. "Possibly. If he had been rushed to the hospital in time." She turned a page. She looked up at Orlando again, and her eyes twinkled. "Here's what's interesting. The razor used to slash his throat wasn't the same one used for the shaving."

Orlando sat back. *Why use two razors?* "How can you tell?"

She raised her eyebrows conspiratorially. "We medical examiners have our ways." Ronnie rose from her chair and went to a huge metal door across the room. Orlando could see this homicide case was beginning to intrigue her. This was the Ronnie he knew.

She lifted the latch and stepped inside. A funny smell wafted across the room to his nostrils. She brought a gurney back into the room and slammed the door shut with her foot. A body in a dark brown plastic bag lay on the gurney.

"It's show time!" Ronnie said wryly. She peeled back the zipper and exposed the stiff corpse of Avraham Rabowitz.

Orlando walked slowly around the gurney, averting his gaze until he stood next to Ronnie. This was something he would never get used to, seeing the dead. The body had been stored in a refrigerated room, and it looked like it.

Ronnie caught his expression. "He won't be winning any beauty contests soon," she murmured. She stooped and gently handled the fingers of the right hand. "Look here. See the different sizes of the lacerations? When I measured the width of the cuts, I figured two razors were used. The one found by the body had a considerably thicker edge than the other."

Orlando bit his lip. Two razors. Only one had been found at the murder scene.

"And see here." She pointed to cuts on Rabowitz's jaw. "The shaving was done with the narrower razor. Not this." She indicated the open gash across the neck. "The razor you found was used here."

So the killer took the razor used for the shaving, but left the one that slashed the victim's throat. Or, as Orlando had surmised the night before, the shaving had taken place earlier at an unknown location, while the throat slashing had occurred in the bedroom.

As the facts sunk in, Orlando jumped with

a realization. "Ronnie, I thought you said Hennessy did the autopsy."

She stiffened, the color draining from her face. "Yes, he did," Ronnie said coldly. She zipped the bag back up with one swoop, the sound having a disturbing ring of finality to it. She rolled the gurney to the door, pulled it open, and disappeared into the refrigerated room.

Orlando stood perplexed. What was going on?

When Ronnie returned, she seemed to have calmed down, but she was all business. She took her chair and studied the report.

"Ronnie, what gives?" Orlando eased into the chair beside her.

Without looking up, she said, "I have to check up on Hennessy all the time. He's sloppy. Nothing would get done right around this place if I didn't watch everybody like a hawk."

They sat in silence. Orlando tried to engage her eyes, but she still refused to look in his direction.

"One last thing," he said finally. "Do you think he was shaved before or after the murder?"

"Before. He washed his face after the shaving. There was soap residue on his cheeks."

Orlando nodded. That held with what he had already suspected.

When he left her, Ronnie was still staring fixedly at the report.

The station house was humming at ten that morning. Word processors clicked in monotonous rhythm as Orlando passed the secretarial center and fit a key in the door to his office. Traces of the words "AIDS DEN" were still scrawled across the door in felt-tipped pen, despite the efforts of the janitor with a scouring pad. Another gift from the guys. A secretary scurried by with an arm load of documents. Two square-jawed rookies in uniform strode down the hall and nodded at him as he looked up from the lock. They were too new on the job to know who he was. They won't be nodding long, he thought.

His office was small and bare, without any attempt to personalize it. Even at home, he left the decorating to Stewart. In reckless moments, he'd considered bringing a framed picture of Stewart to set on his desk like other cops did with their wives and kids. Now that everyone seemed to know, it didn't seem such a radical step. But after the experience with the car, he didn't want to chance it. He knew the lock on his door was no barrier. And if anyone messed with a picture of Stewart, he wasn't sure he would want to be held accountable for what his reaction might be.

His being homosexual had never been much of an issue until the grand jury probe. He'd always been closeted on the force, and though there'd been whispers and titters, it hadn't affected his treatment on the job. Probably because nobody really believed it. He was too good a cop to be seriously suspected of not being one of the guys. But after his testimony,

it all fit together. *The snitch was a queer*. It
made sense. *How could a guy like that be part
of a team? What did those people know about loyalty, the code of ethics that held cops together like
ligaments bind bones?* The whispers and titters
became snickers and open scorn. The word
"faggot" jumped electric from otherwise muffled conversations when he walked into the
station house lounge.

But sometimes, this was preferable to the
stone silence, spreading like a cancer, whenever he entered a room. The wary eyes, the
lips twisted in distrust. He was a threat to
them, the most dangerous kind of cop.

Mrs. Burdict stuck her nose in the doorway
as Orlando settled in the padded chair behind
his desk. She was the secretary for Orlando
and three other homicide cops. Orlando was
her favorite. She never mentioned the mael-
strom of controversy surrounding him, and it
didn't change their relationship. She blinked
through oversized glasses that magnified her
eyes and gave her the look of an inquisitive
fish. Her hair was dyed a red that wasn't supposed to look natural and was held in a bouf-
fant style with a veneer of hair spray. She had
been a secretary with the department for
thirty years, and had been with Orlando for
ten.

"So you found the forensic report, Detective
Orlando?"

The report lay squarely on the blotter. Mrs.
Burdict liked things just right.

Orlando winked. "Thank you, Mrs. Burdict." Their relationship was casual in every way except in the use of names. After ten years, he still didn't call her by her first name.

"Coffee this morning?" Mrs. Burdict didn't seem to mind the chores younger secretaries resented, but Orlando always refused. Stewart had told him, half in jest, that it was politically incorrect to expect such services from secretaries. Still, after ten years of saying no, she still asked each morning.

"No, thank you, Mrs. Burdict. I'll tell you what I do need. Could you get me the police file on Rabbi Rabowitz? Also, I'd like every article from the newspaper file on the rabbi, going back, say, ten years."

She pushed the glasses up on her nose. "I can get you the police file right away. The newspaper stuff will take longer. Some today, some later." She massaged the joints in her fingers.

"How's the arthritis?"

"Bad. You'll get no typing from me today." She peered out the door. "Those girls in the secretarial pool hate me. They say I palm all my work off on them. But I can't help it."

"Don't worry about it," Orlando said. "You've been here long enough. You're entitled."

When she left, Orlando picked up the phone and dialed home. Stewart answered on the third ring.

"So how are the finals going?" Orlando asked. "I'm getting hornier by the day."

"Slowly. Don't expect to get it on until Friday night, if ever. I'm so tired I can hardly think."

"What time did you hit the sack? I found you curled in my arms this morning."

"Oh, a couple of hours after you did. But the neighbor's dog barked for at least an hour. Be sure you bring your Smith & Wesson home tonight. I'll make good use of it." Stewart yawned. "I just got up ten minutes ago."

Orlando fingered the forensic report. He didn't want Stewart to know all the details of the case, especially that he was working with Briggs. He'd never hear the end of it. But Stewart was a treasure trove of information, and he needed to know more about the people he was dealing with. He seldom had contact with the Hasidim in his police work. "Stewart, what do you know about the Hasidim?"

"Nothing really."

"But you're Jewish."

Stewart groaned. "I didn't even have a bar mitzvah! My upbringing had about as much in common with the Hasidim as liberal Christians do with right-wing fundamentalists. All I know about those people is that they dress funny and they're against abortion and terribly homophobic. Which is pretty funny actually. I read an article in the *New York Times* that said the Hasidim have the highest wife beating rate in the country. Seems like they should clean up their own act before telling us how to live. This what your case's about?"

Orlando sighed. This wasn't getting him anywhere. "Yeah, I'll tell you about it later."

After he rang off, Orlando read the forensic report. It told him what he already suspected or knew. The blood splotch on the dining room light switch was Rabowitz's blood. No fingerprints on the murder weapon. No clue as to who the murderer was or why the strange modus operandi of the killing.

Briggs stuck his head in the doorway. "I questioned the men from the rabbi's group. He was at the meeting last night just like Mrs. Rabowitz said. They discussed strategies for repealing the Gay Rights Bill." A contemptuous smile played on his lips, then faded. "Rabowitz left at about eleven-twenty. They never heard from him again." He hitched a thumb in the air. "I'm going to interview the neighbors again. Someone had to see something. You coming?"

"You go ahead," Orlando said. "I've got to study the forensic report."

"Reilly wants us to work together."

"Get out, Briggs. Or I'll have you jailed for vandalism. You think nobody in that neighborhood saw what you did to my car? If I find any witnesses, I'll have your ass."

"You'd like that, wouldn't you?" Sneer.

Orlando rose threateningly from his seat.

Briggs raised his hands in surrender, but he was clearly pleased with his little jab. "I'm leaving."

When Briggs disappeared out the door, Orlando pulled his coat from behind the chair. It was time to hunt suspects, and he wanted to work alone.

CHAPTER 4

The factories and warehouses, silent and gray, looked abandoned, but businesses struggled to survive behind their walls, like the last embers of a fire already spent. Most didn't have signs. There was no need. Those who used the facilities knew where they were and what they offered, and those who didn't weren't likely to in the future. Orlando drove past a broken-down yellow school bus stripped of its front wheels. It bowed in front like a downed buffalo. Tires were piled high where the motor should have been. A bent front door dangled from twisted hinges.

In the next block, a black man with a red cap sat on the steps of a sad brownstone brushing his daughter's hair. A confusion of weeds plagued a yard no bigger than a playpen. Small Hispanic grocery stores cornered every block.

The neighborhood changed. Spanish voices became Yiddish. The streets twisted, old world. Orlando parked his car in the business section of the neighborhood. All faces were white, except those of construction workers in blue hats across the street. Whatever they were building, it would be out of place here. Orlando climbed out of his car and into an Eastern European village of a century ago. Signs in Yiddish hung above doorways. Men wore black felt homburgs, temple curls dangling, long black coats flapping in the wind. Shops were so small, Orlando wondered how they could provide sustenance for customers and a livelihood for the owners. Baby carriages clustered at doorways. Some mothers left their babies outside while they shopped. They weren't negligent; this was a closed community and they felt safe here. Orlando stepped on cracked and jutting sidewalks. The street was dirty, but not with the grime of big city life. It was the dusty dirt of country roads.

Orlando turned up a side street lined with well-maintained brownstones. Strollers in many yards. Absolute quiet, strange for the city. Old women draped bedding out of windows to sun.

Menachem Rabowitz lived in a three-story condominium that spanned half a block. The building was new, its bright red brick not yet faded. Bars covered not only the windows but air conditioners as well. Around the back an eight-foot fence guarded a backyard playground with more tricycles than Orlando had seen in toy stores. He wondered what the impoverished kids in the next neighborhood felt when seeing these treasures through the bars.

The morning paper still lay on the front step. Iron bars protected the front door. Orlando rang the bell. The door opened a crack. Orlando took in Menachem Rabowitz in parts rather than as a whole. Small eyes hid behind spectacles, a massive beard obscured the mouth, a skull cap hugged the thinning hair. He wore a white dress shirt and baggy black slacks.

"Menachem Rabowitz?" Orlando showed his badge.

The man nodded but said nothing. He held the door tightly, like a shield.

"May I come in and talk? I'd like to discuss your brother, Rabbi Avraham Rabowitz."

The intensely nervous eyes flickered uncertainly, then hardened to glass. He nodded again and produced a key to unlock the gate. "Sorry," he said, "but we have to be careful."

"You look pretty safe here."

Menachem Rabowitz looked him directly in the eye but said nothing. He locked the gate again after Orlando stepped inside. The living room was doused in tradition, with portraits of stern old men in traditional garb, antiques handed down from generation to generation, and silver candlesticks on a table, but it also had the airiness and brightness of a new building. Raggedy Ann dolls cuddled in a chair. Toy trucks formed a circle in the corner. Children's voices sounded from the kitchen. Silverware clinked against plates. Orlando was not asked to sit down. They remained standing in the hall.

A squat woman stood hesitantly in the kitchen

doorway, a spatula in hand. Her hair was too coiffed too early in the morning to be anything but a wig. Concern etched her eyes.

"I'll take care of this," Menachem Rabowitz said, and she disappeared.

Orlando cleared his throat. He found being straightforward the best way. "I have sad news for you. Your brother was murdered last night at home by an unknown intruder."

Menachem Rabowitz's jaw dropped almost imperceptibly, then abruptly tightened. He eyed Orlando squarely, glints of light reflecting off his glasses from the hall light above. "I'm not surprised."

Orlando frowned. "I guess I don't have to offer you a handkerchief," he said. He was beginning to understand what Michael Greenberg meant. "You know who might have wanted your brother dead?"

"No one in particular. He was hated by everyone. Some men," Menachem Rabowitz said, "ask for it. My brother was one of those men."

"When was the last time you spoke with your brother?"

He thought for a moment. "I can't really say. A long time."

"Make a guess."

The woman appeared in the kitchen doorway again, her face creased with worry.

"I'll take care of this!" Menachem Rabowitz snapped, louder this time. She slipped from view. "Two years. I haven't seen him since my father died."

"You live four blocks away, and you haven't seen him in two years?"

"Not since he left our sect."

A line formed between Orlando's eyebrows. "But you're both Hasidic Jews."

Menachem Rabowitz let out a long sigh. "I don't have the time to discuss the intricacies of my religion or differences of interpretation with you. There are tens of thousands of us in Brooklyn, with many sects among us. Just because we all look the same to you doesn't mean we are. Leave it at this: as far as I'm concerned, my brother died two years ago, the day he converted, and I have long since ceased to mourn his loss."

"Can you tell me why your brother left?" Orlando dug a pad of paper from his coat pocket.

"We are an unworldly people," Menachem Rabowitz said. "We do not involve ourselves with your politics or your world. We keep to ourselves. My brother was not satisfied with this, the wisdom of our forefathers." He shook his head. "Avraham had to stick his nose in everybody's business, always causing a ruckus with someone. And that obsession of his with homosexuals—what have they to do with us?"

Orlando scribbled on his pad. "So he joined a sect willing to interact with the outside world. Willing to involve itself in the political scene."

"Dedicated to it, in fact. My brother be-lieved that he could change the world, but it was the world that changed him. Now officer, if you don't have any further questions . . ."

"Just one," Orlando said as he was ushered to the door. "Where were you last night around midnight?"

"I was home with my wife." There was a pause, then, "She'll testify to that."

"I'll bet she will."

The sidewalk, smeared with dog shit and littered with crushed paper cups, ended abruptly in a smelly quagmire dotted with rocks to step upon, then started up just as suddenly twenty feet away. The odor of broken sewer main was overpowering. No trees shaded this street; the color scheme was concrete and faded brick. Stoops jutted out from sagging brownstones, flanked by bent garbage cans. Three old black men lounged in patio chairs on the sidewalk, conversing. As Orlando passed them they fell silent, and he felt icy stares rivet onto his back.

He came to a stop in front of a colorless apartment complex in the middle of the block. Dingy curtains hung in the windows. Sooty fire escapes clung to the side of the building like spiders waiting.

Orlando mounted the stairs and pushed through double glass doors smudged with fingerprints and what looked like the dripping remnants of a collision with an ice-cream cone. He made his way to the third floor, the narrow stairs of chipped linoleum whining beneath his feet. A television bellowed through one door. Someone had abandoned a dirty cat box on the second floor landing, and its stench permeated the hallway. Orlando pressed the buzzer beside Donese Jones's door.

He could hear children roughhousing inside, but there was no response. He knocked.

He heard a muffled "Wait a minute" and the sound of heavy feet. The door opened on a chain, revealing a sliver of a woman, eyes hard, skin the rich brown of coffee beans, hair cut short and topped with a red beret.

Orlando flipped open his wallet and bared his badge. "Detective Orlando, Homicide. I'd like to speak with you for a minute."

She looked uncertain. "Look, I just got in. My kids need to be fed." She turned back into the room and shouted, "Duane, you're making a mess! Just eat that ice-cream cone and stop bothering your brother."

"I'll only take a moment."

She wasn't listening. "I'm going to take that away from you, hear? I'm never going to buy you ice cream again if you act like that. And you'd better eat your lunch like you said you would."

He was going to have to lean, and he didn't want to. This woman had been leaned on enough. "It's either here or at police headquarters."

She flashed a look of distrust, then released the chain and opened the door wide. A pit bull resting beside the couch snarled and bounded

toward him. Orlando staggered backward.
Donese snatched the dog's collar, pulling him
back.

"Runyon! Be good."

Runyon rose on his powerful hind legs like
a bucking stallion. His front paws flailed the
air, teeth exposed in a deadly grimace, a gut-
tural noise emanating from his throat. Threads
of saliva drooled from fleshy pink lips.

"You be good!" Donese shouted. "I'm putting you in the bedroom if you act like this."
She yanked him backward, toward the bedroom, but he remained on his back legs, strain-
ing with all his might in Orlando's direction.
"Bad dog!" Donese dragged him into the bedroom and shut him inside. Runyon barked
sharply and scratched at the door.

Orlando felt dizzy. He leaned against the
door frame and let out a sigh of relief. When
a dog like that sunk his teeth into you, he
didn't let go.

"He don't like cops," Donese said, wiping
her hands. "Take your leg off if he thought
you was going to hurt me or the kids. He's
gentle as can be with the baby."

Orlando stepped inside and closed the door
behind him. A frayed couch dominated the living room, surrounded by stick furniture. A
clay figure, made by a child's hands, rested
prominently on the coffee table. There were
no toys in the crib in the corner. A giant water
stain blemished the ceiling. Two narrow windows allowed little light.

Donese Jones picked up her baby, who was crawling on the floor, oblivious to all the fuss. "Whenever I see anyone in this neighborhood with a pit bull, I know he's a drug dealer. They have them to protect themselves from narcs. I figure I might as well have as good protection as they do."

A bony little boy peeked into the room from the hallway, broad brush strokes of ice cream on his face.

"Duane, you wash your face. Look at you. Ice cream all over. You help Brian wash his hands. We're going to have lunch in a minute." The little boy disappeared, yelling, "Brian, c'mere!"

She addressed Orlando. "Kids! I tell you. Why don't you come in the kitchen? These children got to have their lunch."

Orlando followed her past the door restraining Runyon, who had fallen into silence, and the bathroom, where Duane was splashing water on his little brother's hands.

"Boys, wipe up that water on the floor so you don't slip later," Donese said.

The kitchen was small, the Formica table and padded chairs leaving just enough room to maneuver. Finger paintings were tacked to the refrigerator door with magnets. Donese put the baby in a high chair and opened the refrigerator. She found jars of peanut butter and jelly, and set them on the counter. Orlando settled in a chair beside the baby.

"Don't sit there," Donese warned. She smiled

for the first time. "Not unless you want food spattered all over your suit. That baby makes a mess." Orlando moved.

She spread peanut butter on Wonder bread, stopped, and turned, the butter knife dangling from her hand. "Well, are you going to tell me what this is all about, or do I have to guess?"

Orlando leaned forward. "You know that Rabbi Rabowitz was murdered last night."

An incredulous grin spread across her face. "Really? You got to be kidding. No, I hadn't heard."

"You don't read the newspaper? It's on the front page of every paper in town."

"You think I can afford to get the paper delivered?" The baby fussed in his chair. "Don't worry, honey. I'll get your food in a second." She finished making the sandwich, sliced it in half, and placed each piece on a separate plate.

"No, I can't say I heard. Can't say I'm particularly sorry either." She dropped the plates on the table. "You kids! Lunch is on the table." The two boys scrambled down the hall and threw themselves into chairs.

Donese opened the refrigerator again. "You kids want Kool-Aid?" She pulled a pitcher from the rack and closed the door. "This is all I can offer you to drink," she said to Orlando.

"That'll be fine."

She took an ice tray from the freezer and plopped cubes in three Tupperware cups, then poured equal amounts of purple Kool-Aid over each. "After the way that man treated the folks in his buildings, nobody around here going to be mourning *his* loss." The ice cubes rattled in the cups as she placed them on the table.

"These walls ain't been painted in years. That peeling paint could kill my baby. I have to pick it off all the time so the baby don't get at it. I scrubbed the dirt off these walls so long, you can see the color of the old paint coming through."

Orlando tasted the Kool-Aid. He hadn't drunk it since he was a kid. It was much sweeter than he remembered it. He set the cup down.

Donese opened a cupboard above the sink and reached for a jar of baby food. She found a spoon and settled in a chair next to the baby. "All right, honey. It's your turn." She spooned up a mouthful only to have the baby spit it out.

"Rabowitz was murdered about midnight," Orlando said.

She held the spoon in midair. "So you want to know where I was." She shook her head, but she was smiling. "You think I might have done it."

"I don't know. Did you?"

"I'm a suspect?" Donese sat back in her chair and laughed. "Good!"

"You were arrested for attacking him, weren't you?"

"That's not how it happened." She rose and disappeared down the hall, the spoon still in hand. The baby drummed her fists and began to cry.

"Krissy, shush," Brian said. He had finished the sandwich and was wetting his fingers to pick up crumbs on his plate. Duane sat before a half-eaten sandwich, cheeks puffed, looking bloated. Both boys kept their eyes on the table, as if Orlando wasn't there. Orlando had noted that shyness, that distrust of the police, in even the youngest residents of poor neighborhoods before. He wanted to say something reassuring to them, but he couldn't think of anything. After all, he was a cop, and their mother a possible suspect. How were they supposed to feel about him?

"I'm coming, honey, I'm coming," Donese called from down the hall. She whisked into the kitchen, bringing a gentle current of cool air with her. She slapped a photo album on the table in front of Orlando and returned to the baby's side. "I'm here, honey."

Orlando opened the album, and gently fingered through pages of photographs of the boys when they were babies.

"Not there. More toward the end. There's some newspaper articles." She threw Duane a severe glance. "And why haven't you finished that sandwich? I told you when I bought you that cone at the store, you still had to eat your lunch. Now you finish that sandwich this minute or no more ice cream for you."

Duane glumly took a bite in his mouth and played with it with his tongue.

Orlando found two newspaper articles pasted to the back pages of the album. One was a small article from the *New York Times*, the other, longer, was from a daily tabloid and included a photo of Donese shaking her fist. She was wearing the red beret. Orlando looked up to find she still had it on. He wondered if and when she took it off, and what meaning it had for her.

"That article tells it like it was," she said. She spooned another mouthful for the baby.

He scanned both articles. They described what he already knew from the police report. The tabloid story had added comments from Donese, in which she referred to Rabowitz as "the Devil landlord."

"So you read the paper after all."

"When I'm in it, yeah."

"Suppose you tell me what happened."

"He claimed I socked him, but the truth is I didn't touch that creep until he pushed me first. He was on his doorstep, and I admit I was shaking my fist at him, but he shoved me first. Said I was on his private property. Some neighbor called the cops. Both of us were arrested, so you can't say it was my fault. We both dropped the charges against each other. He didn't want any more bad publicity, and I couldn't afford no lawyer."

"You organized a rent strike."

"Yeah, that's how it started. Lot of good it did." She motioned around the room with her eyes. "This place don't look no better than

when we began the strike, and that was over
six months ago. You seen that water stain
thing on my ceiling in the living room? That's
not from rain coming in. That's from the people upstairs' pipes breaking from cold last December. There ain't no heat in this place in
winter. I have to use the gas stove here in the
kitchen to heat the whole place. It smell nasty,
and it's dangerous, too. My kids could die from
that gas. People die that way all the time."

The boys stared at her silently, solemnly.

"You boys, why don't you go into your bedroom and play? And don't let that dog out."
The boys jumped from their chairs and scurried down the hall. "I don't like them hearing
all this stuff. It makes them bitter. I want my
kids strong enough to fight for their rights, but
I don't want them bitter. It's hard raising kids
alone in this neighborhood."

Orlando nodded. "Doesn't their father help?"

"Their fathers ain't around," Donese said
flatly. "I don't need their help. I wanted the
babies, not them, so why should they help?"

Orlando tasted the Kool-Aid again, pursed
his lips at the sweetness, and put the cup
down again.

"Anyway, I got the neighbors together last
fall. We figured we couldn't take another winter without heat, and we'd better organize. We
made out a whole list of demands." She smiled
wistfully, as if she was wiser now. "Like, getting the electric sockets into working order.

None of the sockets work in the living room or bedroom."

"I thought there was a city rental board that took care of things like that. Isn't there a twenty-four-hour number you can call when there's no heat?"

"Yeah, so what? We reported Rabowitz, but it didn't do no good. He got fined once, but that fine wasn't half what it would have cost him to heat this building. Why should he make any changes? When the city let us down, we took matters into our own hands. I hunted down the addresses of all the other buildings he owned in Williamsburg—and he owned a lot. I wrote letters to all the tenants, urging them to join our strike. He had treated them just as shitty as he treated us, and they were glad to join us." She slapped her knee, eyes sparkling. For the first time, Orlando noticed she had beautiful eyes, light brown with hazel chips. "Man! You can't imagine how powerful we felt. For the first time in our lives."

She sat back in her chair, relishing the memory.

"How often did you have personal contact with Avraham Rabowitz?"

"Before the strike, I never even met the guy." Donese raised Krissy from the baby chair in a powerful swoop, and set her on the floor. Standing, she wiped the table and threw the empty baby food jar in a garbage pail under the sink. She cleared the table and began washing dishes, turning her head to the side occasionally to address Orlando.

"The zap squads were my idea. I wanted Rabowitz to know we meant business. The rent strike didn't seem to hurt him and the city didn't seem to care much, so I came up with this idea to hassle him every time he stepped out his door. I didn't want him to be able to go anywhere without angry tenants scolding him for the conditions of his buildings. We drove that man crazy. Think of what it would feel like to have angry people waiting for you to walk out your door, follow you around to the grocery store, the synagogue, whatever, all the time complaining about the water and the heat. That man was never alone. We made his life hell. I scheduled shifts for the tenants to harass him, but in the end, I ended up doing it most of the time. Everybody liked the idea at first, but it can get pretty boring waiting for someone to come out of their house, especially if they stay home all day. After a couple weeks, it was only me. The other tenants got discouraged. It just didn't seem to make any difference. Nothing going to bring heat into this place, except maybe, now that Rabowitz is dead . . ."

She angled the plates on a dish rack, and grabbed a towel to dry her hands.

"So your altercation with Rabowitz occurred during one of your 'zaps'?"

She nodded, somber again, and pulled up

the chair beside him. "Yeah, that must have been two months ago. I ain't seen him since."

"Can you tell me where you were last night at midnight?"

"Here. Alone. Well, with the kids. Sleeping on the roll-out with the baby. The boys have the bedroom." She wrung her hands as if they were still moist. "Look, I don't need no trouble from the police. I didn't kill anybody." Her eyes were soft.

"Have any idea who might have?"

"Sheesh! You kidding me?" A smile broadened her cheeks. "How about everybody? Everybody who knew him, at least. And he knew everybody. I saw him with all kinds of people when I followed him around, and they weren't all Hasidics, either. Bigwigs, politicians, rich people. I even saw him with that guy . . ." She struggled to remember. "He's on the news a lot . . . Leonard Lynch, that's it."

Orlando sat up straight. "Leonard Lynch?" Lynch—a competitor of Donald Trump—was one of the richest men in the city, a real estate mogul of legendary status. Though both were involved in real estate, Rabowitz was worth peanuts in comparison with Lynch, and the two were an unlikely mix. Rabowitz, a religious leader in a black fedora with curled locks at his temples; Lynch, a suave and ruthless businessman as prominent in the social columns and on the boards of city-arts commissions as on the business page and in the backroom dealings of the city's most notorious power brokers. "Are you sure?"

"Yes, I'm sure." She shrugged. "They met a couple times in the weeks I followed Rabowitz around. Rabowitz got smart and started jumping into his car and zooming off whenever he saw me waiting on his doorstep. I ended up borrowing my brother's car to follow him around. He must have thought he had lost me, the way he zigzagged his way to the Upper East Side, but I was there, right behind him. He went into that fancy skyscraper that Lynch built."

Orlando knew the building. It was an extraordinary piece of architecture, Manhattan's newest tourist attraction. Visitors to the city made a pilgrimage to Lynch Towers with the same reverence that they accorded the Empire State Building. Lynch, in characteristic modesty, called the skyscraper a monument to himself. He had gloated that his building made Trump Tower look like a cracker box. The lower portion of the building housed offices, with multimillion-dollar apartments above them. The penthouse, with its expansive view of the city, was reserved for Lynch's offices.

"But that doesn't mean they ever met. Thousands of people enter that building every day. That doesn't mean they have an audience with Leonard Lynch."

"I didn't think twice about him going in that building then. But later, I saw Rabowitz with Lynch right here in Williamsburg."

Orlando gazed at her thoughtfully. Her story seemed less and less likely, but what reason did she have to lie?

"Lynch picked him up in this big fancy limousine. The kind with the windows where you can't see in. But just as the door opened, I got a good look at Lynch's face. It was him all right." Satisfaction colored her face. "And boy, did he look mad that I saw him."

"That was the only time you saw them together?"

"Well, yeah. But they probably met lots of times. I only followed Rabowitz around a short while."

The bedroom door slammed, and Brian stormed into the room. "Duane hit me, Mom!" Duane followed in hot pursuit. "Did not!"

"Both you boys, shush." Donese enveloped them in her arms, gently caressing their close-cropped scalps. She stared off into space. "Don't matter much one way or the other about this Lynch thing." She looked up at Orlando. "Only important thing is this: with Rabowitz dead, maybe now we'll get some heat."

CHAPTER 5

had gotten him past a phalanx of guards on the ground floor. I wonder how much further his credentials would get him. There was the upstairs elevator, he said to mind. Neanderthal operation, a pass with a proper permits in security code and badges.

The reception area of Lynch Enterprises was larger than many museums, and displayed a collection of treasures any curator would envy. Orlando couldn't remember the name of the sculpture that greeted those who entered the offices, nor could he recall the artist's name, but he vaguely remembered photographs of the object in art history books he'd studied in college. And a front-page article announcing its purchase by Lynch for an astonishing sum. Matching medieval tapestries hung on each side of the bank of elevators, blending magnificently with the modern decor of the rest of the room. The statement was simple: the very best, old and new. Soft light filtered down from the two-story ceiling like a benediction on the people below. Floor-to-ceiling windows boasted a stunning view of the cityscape.

Not just anyone could enter the penthouse of Lynch Tower. Employees carried identification cards, and those without proper papers were stopped long before the fifty-story ascent in the elevator. Only Orlando's police badge had gotten him past a phalanx of guards on the ground floor. He wondered just how much further his credentials would get him.

There were guards upstairs, too, but of a different species. No Neanderthals permitted in the penthouse. These guys had class. They wore suits Orlando couldn't afford, would never be able to, unless he won the lottery. They had the air of successful businessmen, and the only way Orlando could tell them apart from the real thing was the watchfulness of their eyes, alert and hard. And of course, bulges in their jackets reflected discreet but unmistakable weaponry. They lounged inconspicuously on luxurious couches or stood by the windows, pretending that they were waiting for an appointment, but their eyes scrutinized every person who came through the elevator doors.

Orlando stepped to the reception desk and showed his badge for the third time since entering Lynch Tower. "Detective Orlando, Homicide. I'd like to speak with Leonard Lynch."

The receptionist furrowed her brow. She was all angles and sharp edges, the paint on her face as thick as that on the Jackson Pollock on the wall behind her. "You have an appointment?" She scanned the appointment book doubtfully.

"This is a police matter. Please tell Mr. Lynch that I'm here." Orlando could feel the eyes of the guards around the room pinpointing the back of his head.

The receptionist rose and turned on her heel. "I'll be back in a moment." Her dress radiated style and swayed with her hips as she disappeared into an inner office.

Orlando read the appointment book upside down. He didn't recognize any of the names, but the fact that there were any indicated Lynch must be in. Casually, he let his hand fall on the book and flipped the page. Again, the names were not familiar. Behind him he heard a guard step closer.

The receptionist returned, face impassive. "I'm very sorry, Detective Orlando, but Mr. Lynch is not in today. Perhaps you would like to make an appointment."

"Do you know when he'll be in?"

"I don't have that information." She looked at the appointment book, saw that Orlando had turned the page, and threw him a glare as sharp as her features. "This is not for you to touch."

"You realize that it's a crime to lie to a police officer. If Lynch is here, I want to see him."

"I'm afraid that isn't possible. I believe he'll be away for the rest of the week." She concentrated on the book. "Ah, here. In two weeks I should be able to fit you in. Thursday, the twenty-first, at three-forty-five P.M."

"That's not good enough. If I walk through that door," Orlando brandished a finger at the inner office door she had used, "and Lynch is in there, I could arrest you, you know."

"I'm afraid we can't let you do that," an authoritative voice boomed from behind him. Orlando spun around. He was surrounded by six guards. They were bigger up close, with barrels for chests and tree trunks for necks. "Not unless, of course, you have a search warrant."

"I was hoping that wouldn't be necessary."

"The lady says he isn't here. If you want to make an appointment, fine. Otherwise, I think you'd better go." The six took a step closer to him in unison.

It was hard for the receptionist to hide her amusement, even under all that makeup. "Do you want an appointment, or not?"

"I think I'll pass. May I use your phone?"

"If you can be brief." She sat down and pushed the telephone toward him.

Orlando dialed his office, then leaned back on the desk, staring eye to eye with the guards. He wanted them to hear this. He knew they would pass it on. He gazed over their heads and saw cameras discreetly hung in the corners of the room. So much the better. Lynch was watching. "Yes, Mrs. Burdict, Orlando here. I want you to do something for me. Check to see if Rabbi Rabowitz filed any papers with the city to change the zoning of any neighborhoods in Williamsburg. That's right. If you need the addresses of the specific blocks, I can get that for you later. And while you're at it, get me everything you can on Leonard Lynch."

Orlando set the phone in its cradle and

thanked the receptionist. As he strode past
them to the elevator, the guards parted as if
they had been trained by a choreographer. He
looked directly into one of the cameras in the
corner.

"I'll be back."

The hole-in-the-wall off State Street served
the best deep-dish pizza in Brooklyn, but the
help behind the counter left something to be
desired. Tony's Pizza was a family-run business, with the mother sitting mute in a chair
by the window—black hair pulled back in a
severe bun—observing customers with the cold
stare of a concentration-camp commandant.
Her teenage daughter, who had recently come
into a full figure and liked to show it, snapped
gum sullenly as she punched the cash register
keys. The son, a few years older and probably
named Tony Jr., sweated in a stained T-shirt,
thrusting pizzas on a huge spatula into a hot
oven like a laborer shoveling coal into a fur-
nace. As far as Orlando knew, Tony never
showed his face in the restaurant.

The lunchtime crowd had cleared, and only
a few people huddled in the vinyl booths. Orlando took his slice and a Coke to the stand-up
bar along the wall. He swallowed a mouthful,
washed it down, but was thinking too hard to
notice how good it tasted. He wasn't sure how
Lynch fit in with all this, but he knew he
would have to confront the entrepreneur eventually. But how? His tenuous connection with

Rabowitz wasn't cause for a search warrant or to bring Lynch in for questioning. An idea occurred to him, but he put it aside for now. Ideas like that got him into trouble.

He finished the pizza and wiped his greasy fingers on a paper napkin. One thing he was pleased about: when he'd slipped into his office earlier to pick up the information Mrs. Burdict had dug from the files, Orlando had successfully avoided running into Briggs. Now if Briggs kept his mouth shut and didn't tell Reilly, maybe Orlando could just solve this case before having to work with that bastard again.

As Orlando crumpled his cup and dunked it in the garbage can, a familiar face appeared against the brightness outside, pushed through the glass door into the dimness of the pizzeria, then stopped. The man's name was Bill Shaw, and he and Orlando had been good friends once. Shaw looked away.

"Don't worry. Nobody's watching," Orlando said with a trace of sarcasm. They hadn't spoken since his testimony. This was a conversation Orlando had wanted to have for a long time.

"It has nothing to do with that, and you know it." Age was beginning to show in the wrinkles around Shaw's eyes and the sprinkle of gray in his tightly curled hair, but he was still handsome.

"All I know is that you ditched a good friend when the going got rough. Don't tell me you don't shake worrying what everyone else on the force thinks."

"Don't blame me because you acted stupid."

"I do blame you. When everybody saw that my best friend in the department wouldn't stand beside me, it was open season. Jesus, Bill, Briggs shot that kid twice in the back. The kid was black. Doesn't that mean anything to you?"

Shaw raised his hand in warning. "Don't try that on me. That's what everybody expects. Just because I'm black, I'm supposed to sympathize with every black cutthroat in the city. Well, I don't. And I resent your assumption." He glanced at his watch. "Look, I don't got time to talk right now."

"Don't let me keep you from your lunch. I was just leaving." When Orlando reached the door, he turned back. "Someday, Bill, you're going to have to decide which side you're on."

"I already have."

But from the tone of his voice, Orlando knew Shaw didn't feel good about it.

You never saw a copy of the *Village World* on any officer's desk. The daily tabloids, yes, sometimes the *New York Times*, but never the *Village World*. Buying a copy of the weekly paper was tantamount to joining the Communist party and dropping one's membership in the Policemen's Benevolent Association on the same day. The police commissioner had labeled it a porn rag after an especially incisive exposé of police-department corruption. The newspaper, with its leftist roots, took a particular glee in examining police abuses.

The paper's offices took up the second floor of a modern building off Fourteenth Street in Manhattan. It was all indirect lighting, stark white walls, and potted palms. Word processors clacked from behind opaque dividers. Orlando told the receptionist that he had an appointment with Herb Chiligny, and she pointed a lacquered fingernail in the direction of his office.

The door was open. Chiligny leaned back in a thickly padded swivel chair, phone at his ear, crossed legs resting on the desk. He raised his eyeballs skyward in exasperation and mouthed the words, "I'll be with you in a moment."

Orlando sunk into an equally padded chair. The walls of the office were hung with beautifully framed original posters from forties *films noirs*. *The Maltese Falcon, Murder, My Sweet, Lady in the Lake.* Some framed copies of the column "Chiligny Maligns" graced one wall. Chiligny held the unusual position at the *Village World* of writing both a very funny gossip column detailing the exploits of the stars and startling articles on New York politics.

The journalist hung up the phone with a flourish and murmured, "I thought *that* conversation would never end." He smiled at Orlando. Chiligny's hair was short and spiky, his skin a rich tan, with brown doe eyes set far apart in a round face. His clothes were stylish, expensive. He looked Orlando over with appreciation, as if he was examining the label of a fine wine. He reached out and squeezed Orlando's hand, holding on to it a moment longer than he had to.

"Well, this is the first time the police have ever come to *me*."

Orlando pulled his hand away.

"So, what can I do for the Brooklyn P.D. this afternoon? I do so love to serve our men in blue." Suddenly he had the appearance of an impish six-year-old, but the lecherous arch of his brows was anything but childlike.

"You can start by cutting the crap."

Chiligny settled back in his chair, like a cat ready to start purring. He wiped the grin off his face, but amusement still danced under the surface. "You have to forgive me," he said, "but I can't help but be tickled pink by your visit. If you only knew my status with the New York Police Department."

"I know your reputation. That's why I'm here."

"Oh, good. My relationship with the boys in blue goes back a long way, you know. To '69, in fact, no pun intended. If I remember correctly, I was first arrested at a sit-in at Mayor Lindsay's office. Something about trying to get the Gay Rights Bill passed, or the sodomy laws repealed, I can't recall which. What I do remember is being repeatedly struck with a nightstick despite the fact that I didn't resist arrest." His features turned savage, and he chuckled sourly. "Of course, that was preferable to the cop who ground my face in the sidewalk when I stepped out of a bar on Christopher Street back in '71. Was that you by any chance?"

"I've never done a thing like that in my life," Orlando snapped. "You should have filed a complaint against those assholes."

"Oh, I did, Detective Orlando." His tone was momentarily sweet. "But there never was much justice in this town for ..." His face twisted and he spat the word out: *"Faggots!"*

Orlando couldn't argue with that. "I didn't come to talk about bad cops." He cleared his throat. "What do you know about Rabbi Avraham Rabowitz?"

Chiligny blinked. "Well, other than that he was a sleazeball? I'm not sure what you want from me. Do you want me to say that I'm glad he's dead? Okay, I'm glad he's dead. Next question."

"You wrote a series of articles about him."

"I wrote a series of articles about attempts to pass the Gay Rights Bill over a period of fifteen years. It was inevitable that Rabowitz was mentioned, since he seemed to dedicate his life to tormenting the gay community."

"Did you know it was rumored Rabowitz was planning a campaign to repeal the bill?"

"He couldn't. It's been part of the city charter since '86, no thanks to him."

"They say he was planning strategies to get around the charter."

Chiligny's voice was ice. "Then it's good he's dead, isn't it?"

Their eyes locked and there was a long moment of silence.

Then Chiligny's expression softened. "Orlando." He rolled the name around on his tongue. "Orlando." He brightened. "I know you! You're the one who testified in the Willis case. That took guts. I couldn't believe a cop would do that. I bet you don't have many friends left on the force."

"Not many."

Chiligny leaned forward, elbows on the desk, fists propping up his chin. "Okay, sorry about the lecture. I thought you were a typical homophobic flatfoot. By the way, I wrote an article on the Willis case. I can get you a copy if you'd like."

"No thanks," Orlando said dryly. "I already know what happened. I want to hear about Rabowitz. I take it you know he was murdered last night about midnight."

"Read it in the morning papers. I can't say the news broke my heart. He was not a nice man."

"Tell me about it."

Chiligny took a deep breath and let it out slowly. He had a list of grievances. "The creep would get his cronies together to counterdemonstrate during the Gay Pride March. Every year he'd join the Catholic bigots across the

street from St. Patrick's, behind police barri-
cades, screaming at us as we marched by. Last
year he had a sign that said, 'AIDS IS GOD'S
PEST CONTROL.' A real nice guy. A barrel of
laughs. Every year he'd bring his friends down
to the council hearings on the Gay Rights Bill
to campaign against it with the right-wing
Christians. I mean, these people would take
the day off from work to testify against my
rights. I remember back in the early eighties,
this Harlem preacher's son got a machine gun
and went on a killing spree shooting up gay
bars in the Village. I testified at the council
hearings that this is where religious bigotry
against gays leads. It leads to murder. When I
mentioned the killings, Rabowitz jumped up
and applauded. The man applauded getting a
machine gun and shooting gays down!"

Chiligny's fist came down on the desk with
an angry thump. His cheeks had taken on
color, and his eyes had taken on fire. When he
saw Orlando watching him, he caught himself
and sighed. "Sorry. I get carried away." He
smiled thinly. "One thing I'll say for Rabowitz, he was an equal-opportunity fascist. Homosexuals weren't the only ones he hated. You
should see the living conditions of the tenants
in his buildings—most of whom are black."

"I have."

Chiligny raised his eyebrows. "Detective
Orlando, you never cease to amaze me. Anyway, last year I was going to include Rabowitz
in my list of the twenty worst landlords in the

city except for the fact that there were other landlords just as bad who owned *more* property. Rabowitz owned a lot of buildings in Williamsburg, but he was hardly a giant in New York real estate."

Orlando remembered the stack of land-option agreements in the rabbi's desk. "Have you any idea where Rabowitz would get the money to buy hundreds of millions of dollars in real estate in Williamsburg?"

Chiligny shook his head. "Rabowitz was certainly worth a lot because of his property, but he wasn't a big-league player. No way could he get his hands on that kind of money."

"What I'm about to tell you is off the record," Orlando said. He waited until Chiligny gave him a nod before continuing. "I found land options in the rabbi's belongings. It looks like he was planning to buy up half of Williamsburg."

A frown creased Chiligny's round face. "Then he must have had a silent partner. I'm sure there's a story in this, but I'm not sure what it is."

Orlando had a good idea who the silent partner might be. But why? Why would Lynch ally himself with a man like Rabowitz?

The telephone rang. Chiligny pressed it to his ear. "Yeah, yeah. I'll have it for you in a few minutes." He set the phone in its cradle. "I have a deadline to meet, Detective." He rose. "Let me walk you to the elevator." Chiligny pulled a cane from under his desk and leaned on it as he walked. He didn't have to look up to see the surprise on Orlando's face. "I've had complications due to diabetes," he said.

He shut the office door behind them and ushered Orlando down the hall. The cane made muffled thumps on the carpet as they walked. "What were we saying? Oh, yes, Rabowitz hated everybody. He was against women's rights, even picketed that abortion clinic in Williamsburg. You know, the one that got bombed on Monday. Used to hang out with his antiabortion cohorts, and harass women as they stepped through the clinic doors. That man spent a lot of time in other people's business."

Chiligny jabbed the elevator button. "Yeah, Rabowitz was a real charmer. I'm sure we'll all miss him."

Orlando stepped into the elevator. "I have just one more question. Where were you last night around midnight?"

Chiligny threw him a grin and said, "Aw, c'mon, Detective. You're not going to go Humphrey Bogart on me, are you?"

The elevator door closed before Orlando got an answer.

The sign said "CLOSED FOR THE DAY—ANOTHER ABORTION CLINIC BOMBING. YOU CAN BET WE'LL BE OPEN TOMORROW." The letters were written with felt-tipped pen and determination. The sign was taped to the door frame. The door no longer existed, just splintered fragments of wood clinging to contorted hinges.

Orlando stepped through the doorway. The room had been a reception area, but it didn't seem inviting now. Debris gritted between his shoes and the linoleum floor. Shards of glass sparkled grimly amid hunks of wood and plaster. Upholstered chairs lay overturned, slashed, guts protruding. The window to the receptionist's office was now a jagged edge of glass.

It looked like the sign was wishful thinking.

The small receptionist's office was a little better off. There was glass, but no other debris. File cabinet drawers were flung open, their contents scattered on the floor. There had been an unfinished attempt to straighten up: a small neat pile of client records lay on the desk like a good deed abandoned.

The rooms where the abortions were performed were all chrome and steel. They looked untouched. The lights were on in all the rooms, but no one was here. Orlando walked back to the front door. He stood for a moment, looking back into the room.

"The sign is wrong."

The voice was deep and feminine at the same time. Orlando turned to find a woman with a broom and dustpan standing in the late-afternoon sun on the sidewalk. She reminded him of a Picasso Madonna. One of those heavy-bodied maternal figures of the artist's neoclassic period. Her nose was large and straight, her hair jet black with a slight frizziness, kept long and simple. There was a healthy shine about her skin, though it was rather white.

"I figured," Orlando said.

"Put it up Monday afternoon. I really thought we'd be in business today, but as you can see ..." She raised the broom and dustpan. "I'm Stacy Black. Who are you?"

He flipped his badge and introduced himself.

"Oh." She glanced away.

"I'm getting that reaction a lot today. Is it something personal?"

"Let's just say I wouldn't mind so much if I knew whose side you were on." As she brushed past him, he smelled the scent of lavender. She began sweeping the rubble. It didn't take long to fill the dustpan.

"What's that supposed to mean?"

Stacy didn't answer, but stepped outside. He heard her empty the debris in a garbage can. When she came back, she gazed at him for a long moment. "You may not know this," she said, "but a lot of the creeps who have been harassing this clinic have been off-duty cops. It doesn't give me such faith in this investigation."

She went back to sweeping. "The investigators took their precious time about looking for clues. I had the feeling they were just trying to keep the clinic closed for as long as possible.

Since when does it take two days to dust for fingerprints?"

"They were probably examining the debris for bomb fragments. That takes time, but it can tell us a lot about who did this."

She scoffed. "Fat lot of good it'll do. Since when have you seen those terrorists get a jail sentence? We already know who did it anyway."

"Who?"

She glared at him as if he were stupid, or playing stupid, then walked outside without a word. Her dustpan banged angrily against the garbage can. When she came back, she said, "You can turn those chairs right side up if you want."

Orlando set a chair on its legs and brushed it off. A cloud of dust mushroomed up. He wiped his hands and said, "Why Williamsburg, of all places? Why open an abortion clinic here?"

"Meaning?" The word carried a sharp inflection.

"You must have known there'd be opposition from the community. This is a Hasidic stronghold."

"Meaning, you think we asked for it." She pointed a menacing finger. "Let me tell you something. They don't own this neighborhood. There are plenty of women here who need our services. Black women, Hispanic women, and yes, Hasidic women. When their husbands aren't looking, they come here to have their abortions. To tell the truth, I didn't pick this neighborhood, it picked me. I just couldn't afford the rents in Brooklyn Heights."

Orlando righted another chair. He didn't know what to say to her. "Looks like this room took it the worst. The rooms in back don't look so bad."

"They did their dirty work there, too," she scowled. "It's just not so noticeable. They bent all the surgical tools, so they'll all have to be replaced. These were clever fellows—they even knew how to dismantle our burglar alarm. And now the insurance company is trying to back out of paying."

"Can you tell me what happened? From the beginning."

Stacy shrugged. "We locked up as usual Saturday afternoon after business hours."

"See anyone unusual around that day?"

"The only unusual people we've seen around here are short little men with long beards in funny black suits screaming at our clients that they're baby killers," she said tartly. She thought for a moment, then said, "Actually, now that I think about it, the Hasidim only bothered us on weekdays. And last week was the first time in a long time there weren't any pickets."

"What happened Monday morning?"

Pain flickered across her face. "Jen came to open up. When she unlocked the door . . ." A shudder rippled through her body, and she turned away from him.

He reached over and touched her shoulder. "You said you didn't know whose side I was on. I want you to know that I'm on your side."

She turned, and he saw there were tears on her cheeks. "I promised myself I'd never let those people make me cry."

She set the broom and dustpan aside, and sat in a chair. She wiped her eyes with her wrists because her hands were dusty. "I just feel so bad because it should have been me. I'm usually the one to open in the morning. I wasn't feeling well, so I asked Jen to do it."

"You can't blame yourself."

She looked at him savagely. "Then who should I blame?"

Orlando raised his eyebrows. "You're the one who claims to know who did it."

She stared sullenly at him, but said nothing. "How is your friend?"

"Well, she's out of shock, and of course she lost her hand. It looks like the forearm can be saved, as long as the doctors can stave off infection. If not, they'll amputate at the elbow." Stacy buried her face in her hands and shook uncontrollably.

Orlando found a box of Kleenex in the receptionist's office and brought it to her. She wiped her face with a fist of tissues, then held them tightly in a trembling hand. "You don't know what it's like . . . seeing her in the hospital. They have her on drugs . . . she can hardly speak. They had to dig pieces of glass and wood out of her face. It's a miracle she wasn't blinded. They'll take her out of intensive care soon. But she'll never be the same." Bitterness twisted her lip. "Jen wanted to be an artist when she was young. She still paints on the side. Painted, I should say."

"I'm sorry."

"She will be, too. Once she's coherent enough to realize what's happened. What kills me the most is these people *wanted* to blow her hands off. They rigged the bomb just right so it would explode the moment she opened the door, right at the level of the doorknob, where they knew her hands would be. They even left a note to taunt us."

Orlando had read about the note in the newspaper. The investigators on the case were still trying to trace it. Letters cut out from newspapers to make up the message. No fingerprints. The cops on the case didn't have to tell Orlando that it offered no real clue to the identity of the bombers.

Her features became wooden as she recited the note: "THESE HANDS WILL NEVER KILL AN-OTHER BABY." She seemed far away for a minute, then demanded in a corrosive tone, "When are you going to arrest the bastards who did this?"

"Actually, I'm not assigned to this case. I'm investigating the murder of Avraham Rabowitz."

She gave him a sour laugh. "Oh, now I see. They bomb my clinic and blow Jen's hand off, and that makes me a suspect in Rabowitz's murder. How typical of the police."

"I never said you were a suspect."

"Then why are you here? 'I want you to know I'm on your side,'" she mimicked him snidely. Her visage turned cloudy, brooding. "Yeah, sure."

"After the bombing, you told the investigators that Rabowitz and his followers planted the bomb. I just read their report. How would you know?"

She sighed. "Look, they were the ones who were always here hounding us. Who else?"

"Can you tell me where you were last night?"

"I was at the hospital with Jen most of the night."

"Most?"

She indicated the remnants of the front door. "Someone had to be here to watch over the place. We took shifts. I was here from ten till two."

"Alone?"

"Alone. Well, I had the company of a .38. The rest of the night I was with Jen or in the intensive care waiting room."

"You know that Rabowitz was murdered at midnight."

"I see." She gave a mirthless laugh, rose, and picked up the broom. She began to sweep. "I think it's pretty clear why you're here. Your kind of support I can do without." She knelt wearily and picked up a chunk of plaster. Her voice had a jagged edge. "Please leave. And don't bother to come back."

He stepped past her and out the door. "I won't," Orlando said. He turned and his eyes were tired. "Unless I've got a warrant for your arrest."

CHAPTER 6

Tuesday night was clear and cold. As Orlando climbed from his Chevy, the air stung his nose and bit his hands. He buttoned his coat and shut the car door gently. He didn't want to disturb the peacefulness of the street. Trees rose above him, branches stripped and gaunt. The sidewalks shone pearl white. Tricycles that sat in the yards in daylight had been taken in, leaving the small patches of grass, blue in the icy glow of the streetlights, lifeless and forlorn. The only warmth in the night came from windows covered with lace curtains too thin to hide families settled in living rooms, books and knitting needles in hand. An occasional wisp of classical piano music drifted down the street.

Orlando looked up to the gaping black windows of the Rabowitz brownstone. Mrs. Rabowitz was staying with her sister's family, the Greenbergs, in Brooklyn Heights. He couldn't blame her. That bedroom would be haunted for her always.

He crossed the street and dug in his pocket

for the keys. Eyes peered out at him from a door studded with window panes in the next brownstone. The door slid open and a man scurried out, arms wrapped around him to guard from the cold. He was bearded and must have been nearly Orlando's age, but dark bangs gave him a boyish look. A yarmulke capped his head. White shirt, trousers black.

"Can I help you?"

Orlando showed his badge.

The man took it in his hands and studied it carefully. He looked from Orlando to the picture in his identification card and back again. "Just wanted to make sure." He smiled apologetically and handed the badge back. "We watch out for one another in this neighborhood."

"Too bad nobody watched a little closer last night."

The man shook his head. "It's a terrible thing. We feel protected here, and safe, even though we know what surrounds us."

When Orlando just stared at him, he continued. "You see, it gets very black several blocks down. They stay away from our stores and the neighborhoods around here. It's not so easy for the people who live in the mixed areas. But around here, they're noticed if they come around."

"Who says the killer was black?"

"Who else?" The man sighed. "Look, I don't mean to come across like some kind of a racist. I'm not. I'm just being realistic. The crimes committed around here are a one-way street. The perpetrators are black, and the victims are Jewish. Period. Ever hear of a Hasidic Jew mugging an old lady?"

"Why didn't anyone see your black murderer last night if everybody's so busy looking out for each other? Even at midnight, someone should have seen something."

"The killer used the back door to the alley."

Orlando smiled. "And how would you know that, Mister . . ."

"Oh, sorry. Sherman. Richard Sherman." He reached out his hand to shake. "A policeman told me. A Detective Briggs. Came around and interviewed all the neighbors. I can tell you nobody saw anything. People don't look out on the alley much. Nothing to see."

Orlando mentally thanked Briggs for his big mouth. "What kind of family are the Rabowitzes?"

"Good neighbors. Quiet. Keep to themselves socially, but of course, the rabbi was rather high profile politically. Mrs. Rabowitz is very shy. Well-behaved kids. Good people." He nodded to himself. "Only problem we ever had was when those blacks from some of his buildings started hanging around to bother him. That was upsetting, having them loitering around. We called the cops several times, but they didn't always come." There was a tone of reproach in his voice. "We even talked about forming a voluntary security patrol for the neighborhood. Actually, it was Avraham's idea. You should have heard what those black activists had to say about that. Now that the rabbi has been murdered, we've finally done what we should have all along. This afternoon the men on our street met and formed a patrol group. We're starting out small, just a group of guys on foot. But eventually we'll get cars with searchlights to cruise the area."

"Big plans." Orlando frowned. "You know, those groups usually just create more tension." This development only promised more problems in solving the murder. "Tell me, did you see Rabowitz return home last night, or hear anything around midnight?"

Sherman shook his head thoughtfully. "Nope. Can't say I did. I was asleep by then. My wife told the police that she didn't hear anything either."

A woman poked her head out the door. "Richard? Shouldn't you have a coat on?" She was short and heavy, with a melodious voice so soft it hardly carried on the wind.

Sherman waved to his wife and turned back to Orlando. "Better get back inside. You know how protective women are." He gave Orlando a sheepish grin. "If you have any more questions . . . ?"

"No. Thank you, Mr. Sherman."

Orlando watched him disappear inside the door, then mounted the steps to the Rabowitz building. There were several keys on the ring Mrs. Rabowitz had handed over the night before. Orlando played with them and the two

bolt locks until the door swung open. It was
dark inside, deathly still. A blue shaft of light
spread over the carpet from the streetlight behind him.

Orlando patted the wall for the light switch,
couldn't find it, and settled on a lamp on the
table. The sickly yellow light of the night before illuminated the room. He pressed the door
shut and felt the aching solitude of the room.

The silence was disturbing.

Crossing the room, Orlando drew the curtain aside and stared out the window. An old
man with a dog strolled down the street. A
light died in a brownstone across the way. Orlando let the curtain fall back in place and
browsed the bookshelves. He didn't recognize
any of the titles—most dealt with religion and
were in Hebrew.

He went to the rolltop desk and flipped
through the stack of papers piled high until
he found the land-option agreements. This
was what he had come for. As he took them
in a fist, several small sheets of paper fluttered
to the ground. He crouched and snatched them
up. The receipts and an uncashed check from
the antique shop on Seventy-second and Madison. He wasn't sure what they were for, but
intuition told him they might just mean something. What had the rabbi been selling? He
settled in a chair by the lamp and began to
leaf through them.

The back of the house creaked.

Orlando froze. Listened. Nothing. He

breathed again. Old houses creaked all the time. His did.

Then it happened again. Floorboards. Back of the house.

He rose and put the papers on the table. The Smith & Wesson fit snugly in his hand. He moved in smooth slow steps, the floor whispering under his feet. The dining room hung with shadows. He flipped the light switch. The dried blood splotch lay on the door frame like a sin unforgiven.

Doors lined both sides of the hall. Orlando assumed firing stance, then threw open the bathroom door. Empty. The master bedroom door was ajar. He kicked it open and slapped on the light. Nobody there. The beds were too low for anyone to hide beneath. He flung open the closet door. Nothing but clothes, Mrs. Rabowitz's and the rabbi's. The dead man's black and white garb hung like patient buzzards.

He passed the kitchen and came to another bedroom doorway. The room was dark, save for a dim carpet of light from the hall. He listened. Silence. Had he just been hearing things? The moment he reached in to turn on the light, an object struck him so hard he stumbled blindly into the room. The gun went flying.

Orlando's head reeled. He swung a fist and hit something solid, but lost his balance. Then he sprawled on the floor, his face digging into the carpet. And everything went black.

He woke in darkness. His head felt like an

overripe melon, soft, squishy. He staggered to his feet. Nausea swept over him, and he curled on the bed, very still.

Finally he got up and turned on the light. His head still felt like a melon. A melon dropped from five stories. The room, he could see, had been ransacked. Children's clothes everywhere: socks, underwear, little trousers strewn on the bed and carpet. Orlando opened the dresser drawers. They were empty. Whoever had been here had cleaned every stitch of clothing out of the drawers and tossed them about the room, then closed the drawers again. Searching for what?

He found his gun under the bed.

The back door was open. The alley was narrow, unlit, paved with brick. The cold of the night soothed his aching head. He checked the lock. No forced entry. That left burglary tools, or . . .

Orlando heard the next door in the alley unlock. Richard Sherman stuck his head out. "I thought I heard . . ."

"It's me," Orlando said. "You didn't happen to hear someone running away a few minutes ago? Maybe a car speed off?"

Sherman shook his head. "I'm not sure. I heard something, but when I looked out, I didn't see anything. Then I guess I heard you fiddling with the door . . ."

"You wouldn't happen to have a key to this door, would you?"

Sherman screwed up his face. "Me? No.

Why would I have a key to the Rabowitzes' door?"

"Sometimes people leave keys with neighbors when they go on vacation, or for emergencies."

"No. They never left any keys with me." He stepped into the dimness of the alley. Arms at his sides, he had a gun dangling from his right hand. When he saw Orlando's stare, his face flushed with a mixture of shame and defiance. "I just bought this today. We have to protect ourselves."

"See that you don't use it on cops in your alley. And don't carry it around with you on your little vigilante squad forays unless you've got a license to pack a gun."

Sherman swallowed hard and nodded.

"I have one more thing to ask you. You're a Hasid, right?"

Sherman shook his head. "Orthodox. There's a big difference. Each Hasidic sect has a rebbe—a charismatic chief rabbi—and what he says, goes. The rebbe is to his followers what the pope is to devout Catholics. These sects go back hundreds of years, to Eastern Europe, and the leadership is dynastic. There are similarities between us, of course. Close families, strong values. They may seem strange to you, but if we had more people like them, we wouldn't have a crime problem in this city."

Orlando remembered Reilly had forbidden him to discuss the case, but in order to get answers, he had to spill a few details of the murder with someone who knew the culture.

"Did you know the rabbi was shaved and the hair is missing? To what purpose?"

Sherman stared. "The murderer must have been crazy. Could the hair have been taken for some cult ritual?"

"Maybe," Orlando said. Or maybe it had just been made to look that way.

CHAPTER 7

Orlando hung his coat in the hall closet. "So how are the illiterate little buggers doing on their exams?" He shoved cheer into his voice and coerced a smile onto his face. He hoped it didn't look like a silent scream. Loose rocks in his skull shuffled with each step. The bump on his head was howling. He had learned in the last year that it was better not to let Stewart know everything that happened to him in his line of work.

He needn't have bothered with the effort. Stewart didn't look up from the test he was grading. "That was last session. This session they know their grammar. They just can't spell." He etched a big red check in a margin with relish and reached for a cigarette.

"I wish you wouldn't."

"I can't help it." Stewart stared. "God, you look like something the cat dragged in. What happened?"

"Nothing. Long day."

Stewart exhaled a plume of smoke. The air was thick. "Sorry about the haze. You know I'm a wreck during test week."

"Yeah, test week," Orlando grunted. He was feeling a little better. Stewart did that to him. This was a scene they had played out before. Seriously once, but now with an ounce of parody. "You taste like an ashtray, and I get cut off for a week."

Stewart gave him that look with those blue eyes. The look Orlando had fallen in love with when they first met. Amusement rippling beneath a placid surface. "Aw, c'mon, it's only a week. And this way, you appreciate me all the more when it's over. And anyway, if I cut you off, how would you know what I taste like?"

"I know because." Orlando hovered over Stewart's chair and planted a fist on each armrest. He stole a slow kiss.

"Now, that wasn't so bad, was it?" Stewart set the cigarette in an ashtray and wiped his glasses on his shirt. "You got me steamed up. Oh, while I remember. Your mother called. She wants you to paint that kitchen before the new tenant moves in."

"I'll do it Saturday."

"She said they're moving in Friday."

"Great. Can't you do it?"

Stewart pointed to a stack of tests. "We always come back to it, don't we?"

"Test week," Orlando muttered. "Tell her I'll try to get around to it tomorrow night." He went into the bathroom. He needed something for his head.

He downed a couple aspirins. That would be

good for starters. He examined his reflection in the mirror. The lump on his head peeked through his bald spot. Great. Why did he put himself through all this grief?

"If I know your mother," Stewart called, "she'll telephone before the evening's out."

The dishes piled haphazardly in the kitchen sink were beginning to smell. Orlando dug ice cubes out of the freezer and wrapped them in a towel. It was a little late to keep the swelling down, but the ice numbed the throbbing. He stayed in the kitchen. He'd just as soon Stewart didn't know about this.

It had been different when they met, twelve years ago. Orlando was still a beat cop then, and Stewart had been taken with his uniform. The blue tapered shirts, the trousers tight in the buttocks. The spit shine on the black holster and shoes. In those days, things like that impressed the men in their crowd. And Orlando had used it, used it to get admiration in bars, used it as proof of sexual prowess. Used it to get beautiful men who wouldn't have looked at him twice otherwise. Beautiful men like Stewart, with his baby blue eyes and fine, striking features. And when they lay together, snug and tight, sheets rumpled and damp, the stories of his work had brought a glow of awe to those blue eyes. It was a look Orlando never wanted to lose.

There was something both profound and rawly sexual in sharing the fears and frustrations of the beat, and Stewart had responded with both caring and undisguised arousal. They had played the games that young lovers play, and sometimes his cap or nightstick found its way onto the sweaty sheets. After they took up housekeeping together and Orlando left the beat for Homicide, the fantasy may have diminished, but did not die—age just softened it. Fiery passion and striving to smash limits gave way to deeper, perhaps less ardent closeness. But those fantasies, like old friends, still popped up now and then, bringing with them the charm of nostalgia.

What was important to Orlando was the pride Stewart felt for him. He had risen to a place of respect in a profession that despised their kind, had fought to get where he was. And Stewart liked fighters. He himself had started his career as a high school teacher at a time when a mere suspicion of his sexuality would have ended in dismissal. He had worked his way up to a professorship at NYU with a stature in the academic community no one dared question.

Then the fantasy died. The cop stories no longer a sexy game, a fantasy to enhance bedroom antics. Orlando's job had become dead serious. Ugly. The grand jury investigation had done that. And what had happened since. At first he had only Stewart's sympathy. The vandalism of his office door. The icy stares of his coworkers. Then, subtly, Stewart changed. Fear crept into their bedroom discussions. He could see it in his lover's eyes. Stewart no longer wanted Orlando to fight; he wanted him to get out. Before it was too late. And what had once been an aphrodisiac became a wall between them. Where sympathy had once been offered, he now got stony silence and gentle reproach. And he couldn't answer Stewart's prodding question: Why stay on? Why?

Orlando dumped the ice cubes in the sink and set the towel aside when he heard footsteps in the hall. Stewart leaned in the doorway. "How about some popcorn? I could use some empty mindless calories to counteract the profundity of these essay answers." He smacked a test against the door frame.

Popcorn drenched in butter was a nighttime ritual around their house. Usually they curled up like a couple of lazy cats on the couch, the bowl of popcorn in front of them, an old movie on the tube.

Stewart shook his head. "They memorize exactly what I say in class, and feed it back to me word for word. It's kind of scary. I never realized what I say would have such effect until I became a prof."

"Sounds like a sincere form of respect to me."

"Or vacuous flattery. I'm not sure which. I'd prefer the little buggers think—why is your hair all wet?"

Uh-oh. Orlando prepared for the storm.

Stewart came over. His eyes widened. "You've

got a knot on your head the size of a golf ball. What happened?"

Their dog, Poindexter, waddled into the room and stared up with accusing eyes. A second member of the inquisition.

"Would you believe my husband beats me?"

"One of your pals on the force didn't jump you, did they?"

"Not so far as I know." Orlando pulled a jar of popcorn from the cupboard. "More likely it was a crazed razor-wielding rabbi killer who would have been much more interested in me if I had a beard to sacrifice."

"Rabbi . . . ?" Stewart mulled it over. "You're on that Rabowitz case? But Briggs is assigned to that one."

Orlando found their blackened popcorn pot and set it on the burner. The storm was brewing. Slow and easy at first, with just a hint of tension. "How do you know that?" He said it casually.

"That brain-dead moron was on the evening news talking about the case. Why the fuck—"

Orlando looked like he'd just drank sour milk. "It's Reilly's little joke. To get my goat. He's tried everything else. I have to say this ploy is a stroke of genius."

"It's not funny. You know what Briggs is. You've got to get out of that place. There are other things you can do."

Orlando let out a groan. The storm was headed directly his way. *Get to the cellars.*

"I'm a forty-two-year-old man. It's too late to change careers now."

Poindexter began to bark, deep-throated, resonant. Every argument in this house had three voices. Each bark shifted the loose rocks in Orlando's head.

"You could do private detective work."

"Chasing runaway husbands? No thanks."

"What about taking over for your mother? She'd love that. She can't care for all this property by herself. We end up doing all the work anyway. Your sister and brother never lift a finger to help her. Retire. Take what pension they'll give you. Then manage your mother's property for her."

"Painting kitchens and collecting rent is not my idea of a stimulating career."

Stewart touched the bump on Orlando's head. Gently. Eyes weary with concern. "That kind of stimulation you could do without. Let me get you some ice."

"It's in the sink."

Orlando bribed Poindexter to shut up with a dog biscuit from a rumpled bag under the sink.

The telephone rang. *Saved by the bell.* Orlando grabbed the receiver from where it hung on the wall. "Oh, hi, Ma. No, no problem. Actually, you're saving me from the clutches of the mad career counselor."

"Very funny. I have a career for you," Stewart said, wrapping the half-melted cubes in the towel. "Stand-up comedian."

Orlando nodded into the phone. "Hold a sec, Ma. I'll ask." He put a hand over the mouthpiece. "She knows what a busy boy I am. She wonders if you could paint 'de kitch'."

Mrs. Orlando had never really learned English in the first three decades since she had left Italy, until Stewart pressured her into taking a series of English-as-a-second-language classes after the death of her husband. She had improved remarkably in the past few years, though her accent hung on. Even now, they liked to kid about the way she used to talk.

Stewart pointed to the test lying on the table. "No way. You paint 'de kitch'."

"It's exams week, Ma. He's up to his armpits in paperwork. The house is a shambles. Dishes in the sink. And I'm not getting any . . ." He looked pointedly at Stewart, ". . . home-cooked meals. I'll try to do it tomorrow night, okay?" They talked about her bad back for a minute, then he rang off.

"Round two," Stewart said. He clinked a dirty spoon against a dirty glass.

Orlando found a block of butter in the fridge. Popping corn did wonders to kill conversation. He quickly lopped off a hunk of butter in the pan and turned on the gas. Stewart stood close, wrapped an arm around Orlando's waist from behind, and held the ice pack on his head.

"I like you better when you're nice," Orlando said. "Truce?"

"Until the corn's popped."

When the popcorn began to explode, Poindexter sauntered down the hall, tail between his legs. Good, Orlando thought. Now the sides are even. After the last kernel shot off, he set the overflowing bowl of popcorn on the table and poured melted butter on top. He always made more than they could possibly eat. They sat at opposite corners of the table. Two boxers in the ring, waiting for the bell.

But Stewart didn't say anything. He munched lazily on popcorn. He seemed far away, pondering. "Maybe we should get away. Go to a beach resort in the Bahamas."

"One of those queenie resorts with all the muscle boys posing on the beach?" Orlando immediately regretted his words. Stewart was reaching out. Why was he cutting him off?

"What's wrong with that? I for one am not too old to appreciate a muscle queen."

They were quiet for a long time; the only sounds were the tick of the clock on the wall and the crunch of popcorn. Finally Stewart spoke. Quietly. "You're not going to find him, you know."

He didn't have to tell Orlando what he was talking about. Orlando knew. The reason he refused to quit the force.

Stewart's eyes were kind. "You're not going to find the guy who killed your dad. You think if you just keep at it long enough, you're bound to run across him. But you won't, Doug. That was ten years ago. You have to put it behind you."

Bull's-eye. That stung. It stung because it was the truth. Who was it that said the eye of the storm was calmest? The simple facts of the matter laid bare made him cringe with humiliation. It seemed such a childish reason to be going through all this. In all these years, it hadn't really occurred to him that he had never wanted to work in Homicide, not until his father's murder.

"I'm sorry," Stewart said. "But I had to say it. You're killing yourself over something you can't do anything about."

Orlando swallowed hard and shook his head. "That's not why." But his voice lacked conviction.

"Then why? Tell me. I'd really like to know. Give me one good reason why you stay on. I'd like to think there's a purpose for all this misery."

Orlando opened his mouth to speak, but nothing came out.

The popcorn caught in his throat.

CHAPTER 8

When Lieutenant Reilly got mad, his cheeks puffed up like a blowfish. His face turned red and a dark road map of tiny veins networked across his cheeks. The white eyebrows descended, and his blue eyes became shadowy pools of anger. "What the fuck were you doing at Lynch Tower yesterday?" he shouted. The door to Orlando's office, which he had just thrown open, banged against the wall. Outside the door, all typing in the secretarial center stopped. Faces with sagging mouths gawked. Then the chatter of typing began again just as suddenly. Reilly left the door open. Orlando guessed the lieutenant wanted everybody to hear this.

Orlando leaned forward in his chair. There were four neat piles on his desk. The land options. The receipts from the antique shop. Rabowitz's police file. And a stack of newspaper articles on the rabbi's exploits. Orlando set his coffee cup down. The coffee was good this morning. Good until Reilly barged in. "What's the problem?"

"What's the problem? I have people to answer to, that's the problem." Reilly seemed to be doing a war dance with his feet. "And I can't have bearded ladies like you mincing around Leonard Lynch's office causing trouble."

Orlando took a long sip of coffee. "You assigned me to the Rabowitz case. I seem to remember a phone call after midnight Monday night. You ask for my services, you get them. Got it?"

"What the fuck do Rabowitz and Lynch have to do with each other?"

"They were seen together."

"Yeah? By who?"

"A young black woman from one of Rabowitz's buildings. Donese Jones. She was following Rabowitz a few months back—"

Reilly's face turned purple. The veins gorged. "A goddamned fucking nig—" he yelled, stopped, kicked the door shut, hissed: "A goddamned fucking nigger tells you she saw them together, and you play storm trooper in the office of one of the most powerful men in the city. You dumb fuck. I oughta have your badge." Reilly's vocabulary went to hell when he got mad. But he was more than mad now, he was afraid.

"'People to answer to,'" Orlando said. "Like who?"

"Like the mayor. Lynch called the mayor after your little run-in in his office. The mayor called the commissioner, and I got a call not ten minutes ago. My ears are still burning."

"I don't care who Lynch's friends are. This is a murder investigation, and I'm in charge. And I'll ask questions of whoever I choose."

"You'll lay off Leonard Lynch, and that's an order."

Orlando picked up the stack of land options and slapped them back down on the desk. "Before he was murdered, Rabowitz optioned millions of dollars' worth of land in Williamsburg. He didn't have that kind of money. I want to know why he did it, and for who. I think Lynch has the answers."

Reilly shook his head. The bulldog jowls kept wagging even after the head stopped. "There's only one thing I want more than getting you the hell out of my life, and that's retiring next year without a hitch. So you stay the hell away from Lynch, hear?"

"Have you ever asked yourself why Lynch is so intent on not wanting to be questioned? Think about it."

"I'm not paid to think. You were supposed to work with Briggs. While he was interviewing possible witnesses in the neighborhood, you were gossiping with welfare mothers and strong-arming the secretaries of city leaders."

"Briggs hit a dead end. I didn't. Lynch's call proves that."

Reilly grabbed the doorknob with stubby fingers and flung the door open. "You'll stick with Briggs from now on, like gum to a shoe, you hear? Like gum to a shoe." He stormed out of the room.

Taking the coffee cup in hand, Orlando remembered what Stewart had said the night before. Was there a good reason for putting up with all this bullshit? He couldn't think of any.

When Orlando downed the last of his coffee, Briggs stuck his head in the door. "Hear you made quite an impression with Leonard Lynch." He chuckled. "Smart move, guy."

"What do you want, Briggs?"

"Haven't you heard? You and me are a team again. Partners. Sidekicks. Buddies. Just like old times." He grinned. "I'm off to see the widow at her sister's place. Coming?"

Orlando grabbed his coat. "Like gum to a shoe," he sighed.

They took Briggs's car. Orlando thought it best not to let Briggs know where he parked his Chevy. Not after Monday night. Briggs turned up Court Street. Traffic inched along through a series of lights. Brooklyn Heights was bustling. Harried employees scurried out of the district attorney's office, nervously checking their watches. Jehovah's Witnesses stood guard at the corner, raising their publications like a shield, faces bland. No one seemed to notice them. Street vendors neatly laid out books on worn blankets. Some people stopped to browse, obstructing the flow of pedestrians. Scaffolding hugged dirty buildings, the clamor of the construction workers drifting down to street level where it merged with the din of horns and blustering engines.

Briggs rolled down the window. Orlando smelled car fumes in the brisk air.

"Old man gave you a hard time, huh?" Briggs grinned. He talked as if they were old friends. "Don't be so down in the mouth. I'm not that bad, am I?"

Orlando didn't answer. Why was Briggs trying to be nice? He stared out the window at a street person in shaggy clothes standing in a doorway, his back to the street.

"You think I'm a monster, don't you? I'm not. I'm just a regular guy." He stopped at a red light, and looked over at Orlando. "Got a wife, kids, the whole bit. Just like a real person—" He stopped. "Hey, that wasn't meant as an insult. I don't care about you being, you know, the way you are. I don't particularly think people like you should be cops, but I don't really care what you do, you know? Just so long as you don't spread any diseases around."

The light turned green. A puddle formed around the street person's feet, and he turned, zipping up his pants.

Briggs stepped on the gas and flipped the turn indicator. "But there are certain things you don't do. Like, you don't fink on other cops. If cops can't stick together, who can?"

"You tell me. And while you're at it, tell the cop who vandalized my car."

Briggs grimaced. "You really don't get it, do

you? You talk about your car. What about my life? I got a wife and kids to support, and you try to send me to Rikers. What would have happened to them if you'd succeeded? I don't take kindly to people who fuck with my family."

"What about the Willis kid? What about his life?"

Briggs slammed his fist on the steering wheel. "A punk with an arrest record from here to Albany. You never think about all his victims, do you? That punk would have killed somebody by twenty, I guarantee you. It's guys like you that make it hard for cops on the street."

"No, Briggs. It's cops like you that make it dangerous for us to be alone in black neighborhoods. Cops like you give us a dirty name. You may think it's funny for me to say this, but your problem is you're too emotional."

Briggs turned down a residential street. Neat brownstones fenced in by black wrought iron. Window boxes. Narrow sidewalks of crooked cement slab, cracking where tree roots had worked their way under them. Briggs stared ahead. "Tell you the truth," he said quietly, "I don't even remember why I pulled the trigger. I just remember how hot it was, and how my shirt was sticking to my back. It seemed like the pavement was steaming up through my shoes. And then I just fired. It was like it wasn't even my hand pulling the trigger. It was like I wasn't even shooting a human being."

Like a wounded animal, Orlando thought. He wondered if Briggs would mention the second bullet.

"It's something that just happened. I don't feel good about it." He turned his head and locked eyes with Orlando. "But I don't stay awake nights over it either. Only thing that cost me sleep was what you did. My wife cried every night, she was so afraid I'd go to jail."

"Don't you think Willis's mother cried?"

"Those people always carry on when their kids get shot by the police. Usually in front of T.V. cameras."

"Your sensitivity moves me to tears, Briggs."

They found a parking spot up the block from the Greenberg home. As Briggs got out, he pulled off his coat and laid it on the seat. "It's warming up." He waited for Orlando to do the same, and when he didn't, Briggs slammed his door and they started down the sidewalk.

Michael Greenberg was standing at the curb, staring. He had a gushing green hose in his hand and a bucket of sudsy water between his feet. He wore a gray jacket daubed with splotches of paint and rumpled trousers that were too loose even for his portly waist, cinched tight with a leather belt. Even in ragged clothes, he had an air of authority. Water cascaded from the roof of his Mercedes.

A sulky teen, hair stringy and long, crouched down, scrubbing a hubcap with a fat sponge. He wore no jacket, just a T-shirt with a heavy-metal band insignia and worn levis that were wet at the cuff. His nose was long and thin, like his body. He shared no physical features with his father. Orlando wondered what Mrs. Greenberg looked like. A little boy, no more than six, sat alone on the steps of the brownstone, bundled in a puffy coat with a hood pulled tight.

"Hello officers," Greenberg said. His tone was friendly enough, but his eyes were wary. He looked back to the little boy on the steps. "Probably getting a little cold out here, Yakov." His voice had a false heartiness that could only fool a child. "Why don't you go ahead inside?" He turned to the teen. "David, why don't you take Yakov inside? Play with him."

David straightened. He must have been over six feet. His shoulders were slumped, his hips tilted in silent defiance. Water dripped from the sponge hanging from long thin fingers onto his sneakers. "I thought you said I had to help you wash the car before school."

"Just go ahead. Take Yakov inside."

David tossed the sponge into the bucket and sudsy water splashed on his father's pant leg. The teen took two steps, then turned back to his father. "I can't be late for school taking care of Yakov. Mom's going to have to do it."

Greenberg nodded, but his face colored with anger. His cheeks seemed to grow fatter. He watched his son take the boy by the hand and lead him inside. The door closed with a bang.

Greenberg shook his head and smiled feebly. "Kids at that age. They think they're so smart. I can't even get him to wear a jacket in this weather." He sighed and gave them a wistful smile. "Adolescence. One day they're bringing home A's on their report card and watching reruns of the *Brady Bunch*, and the next it's satanic music and greasy hair."

Briggs made a noise of agreement in his throat.

"The little boy, Yakov," Orlando said. "That's the Rabowitzes' child?"

"Yes. I didn't want him to hear us. He doesn't seem to understand that his father is gone for good. I don't think at that age they can understand permanent loss."

"You're keeping them home from school?" Briggs asked.

"For the week, yes. Yakov is in the first grade. Rachel is a kindergartner, but she has a bad cold anyway. The youngest is just three. I'm taking the week off myself. I have a partner in my practice, so it's not so bad." He set the end of the hose in the gutter and stepped through a wrought-iron gate into a small patch of cemented-over yard. He twisted a knob until the water stopped.

"It's been a terrible strain on us. Especially Sarah. Imagine finding your husband like that." He shook his head. "I've had to keep her sedated for two days now."

"Can we speak with her?" Briggs said.

"She's been sleeping all day. I hate to give

her so much medication, but she's hysterical otherwise. It's been tough on my wife, too, watching after Sarah's kids as well as our own brood." He dropped the sponge on the sidewalk and picked up the bucket. "You have questions for Sarah?"

"We just wanted to check in with her to see if she had anything else to tell us," Orlando said. "Sometimes witnesses remember details after the initial shock has worn off. When will she be able to talk to us?"

Greenberg looked doubtful. "Depends. Tonight maybe ... tomorrow ..." his voice trailed off. He tilted the bucket, and water streamed into the gutter. "Did you talk to the brother?"

Orlando raised his eyebrows. "Menachem Rabowitz? Yes. Friendly fellow. Do you suspect him?"

Greenberg dropped the bucket. "Oh, no. I hardly know him. It's just that ..." He set the sponge in the bucket and put it in the yard.

Orlando searched the doctor's face. "We'd appreciate any information you can give us."

Greenberg smiled thinly. "Well, you know, they didn't exactly get along."

"That doesn't make him a murderer."

He lost his smile. "No. Of course not." He began to wind up the hose after shaking out excess water. "Of course not." When he was finished, he hung the hose over the spigot. He brushed off his hands. "I didn't mean to point a finger, I just wanted to help. I see from the papers that no one has been arrested."

"Not yet," Orlando said. "Can you think of anyone who would have wanted to kill your brother-in-law?"

"Well, he was a controversial fellow ..." Greenberg blinked thoughtfully. "Wait a minute. Something happened last week that might interest you. A boy who worked for Avraham was accused of stealing. Drugs, I think. Yes, a boy Avraham hired to do some work in one of his apartment buildings was accused of stealing drugs from one of the tenants' medicine cabinets. Avraham fired him on the spot. The kid threatened to get him back."

"You know the boy's name?" Briggs leaned forward.

Creases appeared between the doctor's brows. "Let me think. The boy had done work for Avraham off and on for several years. Avraham was very disappointed because he trusted the kid. Rodriguez, I think. Yes, Jimmy Rodriguez. He lives three blocks south of Avraham's house with his mother. The father ran off years ago, and Avraham took pity on the kid and gave him some work now and then. Maybe this is how the kid paid him back."

"Jimmy Rodriguez," Orlando said. "Thanks."

The boy's eyes were narrow slits in the brightness of the day. He lounged on the stoop of the brownstone, elbows leaning on the gum-scarred landing. He sported an adolescent mustache, soft hairs that looked like a smear of newsprint. He appeared peaceful in the coolness of the sunlight, despite the pounding drive of the rap music shouting from the ghetto blaster beside him. His red T-shirt rode high, and an exposed belly button drifted on a flat stomach as he breathed. His blue jeans were ripped at the knees.

"Are you Jimmy Rodriguez?" Orlando asked. Briggs's shadow fell on the youthful face.

The slits opened slowly, then closed again. He jerked a thumb. "Upstairs. Top floor."

Briggs grunted. "Are you sure you're not Jimmy Rodriguez?"

The brown eyes opened and glinted contempt. "That faggot, man? Whataya think I am? I told you. Upstairs." The eyes slitted again. The song changed but not the monotonous beat. He made no attempt to move out of their way, and they stepped over him and the radio to get to the open front door. Briggs turned back, squatted, and looked at the radio. Orlando glanced over his shoulder. The front looked like the control panel of a jet. Briggs found the switch he wanted and the music died.

"It's against the law to play that thing so loud. Next time I'll give you a ticket and take your fucking toy away."

"Oh, man," the kid said, his face distorted with scorn.

The hallway, dark and narrow, smelled of

cilantro. They trudged up the stairs. Orlando banged on the door on the top floor.

There was a pause, then, "Who is it?" The voice was thick with Spanish accent, female, middle-aged.

"Police. We'd like to talk with you, Mrs. Rodriguez."

The woman said something in Spanish, in low tones, to someone in the room. The television was on.

"We need to speak with your son."

She was at the door now, but didn't open it. "He's not here."

"Just open the door," Orlando said.

"I'm afraid. I don't know who you are." The voice was a whine.

"Open the fuck up or we'll break the door down," Briggs thundered.

Orlando was beginning to remember why he had worked so hard to get out of being Briggs's partner years ago. He threw Briggs a savage glance. He took his badge and slid it under the wide space between the door and the planks of the floor. "My badge, Mrs. Rodriguez. Detective Orlando, Homicide."

Locks unbolted. The door creaked open. She held the badge in beefy fingers. She was large and motherly in an oversized bathrobe. "I'm sorry. I don't have one of those . . . you know."

"Peepholes?"

She nodded and returned the badge. Her eyes still said fear. Cooking smells, mingled with a familiar odor Orlando couldn't define, wafted toward him through the open door. She stared at Briggs with suspicion and dread. "He a cop, too?"

"Both of us." Orlando could see that he would be the one asking the questions—Briggs had already blown any possibility of a civil conversation with this woman. His look told Briggs to shut up. "We're looking for your son, Jimmy. Where is he, Mrs. Rodriguez?"

"Gone," she said, waving them inside. She turned the bolts again. "Please," she said, "sit."

Orlando and Briggs sank into a lumpy old couch. A frail old woman sat stiffly in an armchair in front of a TV set with rabbit ears. Young lovers in a soap opera promised to love each other forever.

"Mama," Mrs. Rodriguez said, "I'm going to turn this off while the police are here, okay?" She spoke in a loud voice, but gently. Orlando thought she was speaking in English for their benefit.

"We don't mean to disturb you. We only have a few questions," Orlando said.

"It's not important," she said, indicating the soap opera, and switched the set off. She watched the tube go gray, as if to see the last traces of the drama, and Orlando got the feeling the program was important to her and that she was trying to hide it. He liked her better for it.

She held her bathrobe tightly at the neck. "I'm sorry I'm not dressed. This morning I bathed mother, and I'm a bit behind." She gave a brief smile, a mixture of embarrassment and shyness. "Let me put on something quickly." She looked back at her mother, then disappeared from the room. The old woman continued to stare at the darkened television.

Orlando took in the room. The walls hadn't been painted in years, and discoloration from scrubbing off handprints plagued the areas around the light switches. Orlando recognized the odor he noticed when Mrs. Rodriguez had opened the door. Mildew. Inside the walls probably. Shafts of sunlight streamed in from tall windows and splashed on floorboards painted dark brown. The place was shabby, but immaculate. A framed picture of Jesus hung on the wall—the same image of Christ Orlando had on his bedroom wall as a kid. Finely knotted doilies spread on the armrests, only partially covering the worn spots. An afghan dropped autumn colors over the back of the couch. Orlando fingered the afghan. The craftsmanship was dazzling.

"That was the last afghan Mama made before the stroke." Mrs. Rodriguez stood in the doorway. She had on the dress she probably wore to church on Sunday.

"Beautiful," Orlando said. Briggs impatiently drummed his fingers on the armrest. "Yeah, real beautiful."

"The doilies are Mama's, too, but she hasn't done that in years, even before the stroke. Arthritis. But she kept on with the knitting right up to the stroke. It's been . . . almost two years now." She raised her hands to indicate tin-craft star bursts hanging on the walls. Her arms were big, not from muscle, but fat, which hung and jiggled when she lifted them. "And she did these, years ago. From tin cans. Aren't they beautiful?"

They were.

She stood by her mother and stroked her hair. The wispy white hair was plastered back, the pinkness of the scalp exposed. "It's been hard on Mama, these last years."

The old woman mumbled something in Spanish, but Orlando figured that if he knew the language, he still wouldn't be able to understand her. But Mrs. Rodriguez responded, like a mother who can understand her baby's babbling.

"You're hungry, Mama? Okay, just let me get something." She turned to the men. "How about if I make you some fresh-ground coffee?"

As she disappeared, Briggs grinned. "Beans, beans, beans. These people are always doing something with beans." Orlando eyed him with disgust, then glanced at the old woman. She seemed oblivious to Briggs's comment.

A few minutes later, Mrs. Rodriguez came back with a tray and set cups in saucers on the coffee table in front of them. She pulled up a wooden chair and sat in front of her mother, the tray on her lap. She tucked a bib in the collar of the mother's dress and began to spoon-feed mush from a bowl that matched the coffee cups. "Jimmy's been gone since last Saturday," she said without looking at them. "Visiting cousins in Puerto Rico."

Orlando sipped the coffee. It was strong, fragrant. "Since Saturday. He doesn't have school?"

Mrs. Rodriguez looked at him with weary eyes. "Not anymore." She gave her mother another spoonful, then daubed with a napkin at her mother's chin. "Two years to go, only two years, and he drops out. I begged him not to do it. Now what can he be?"

"At least he got work, that's better than most dropouts."

"Sometimes he works."

"How often did he work for Avraham Rabowitz?"

Her body stiffened, and she quickly spooned another mouthful from the bowl. "How is that, Mama? Good?" She turned to Orlando. "He did little things for the rabbi over the years. Some painting. Cleaning up apartments after tenants moved out."

"You know Rabowitz fired him last week."

Mrs. Rodriguez dropped the spoon in the bowl. "Oh no. He quit. The rabbi didn't pay enough. He was offered a better job."

"Where?"

Fear had returned to her eyes. "In Bensonhurst. A friend in Bensonhurst gave him a job."

"Mrs. Rodriguez, Jimmy was fired for stealing." Orlando set the cup in its saucer.

She shook her head vehemently. Her accent became stronger. "Not my Jimmy. He doesn't steal. He has no direction, but he's not a bad boy."

"He stole drugs from a tenant's medicine cabinet."

"No, not drugs. He's not like that."

Briggs scowled. "Look lady, we just checked. He's been arrested for stealing before. And possession of drugs."

The brown eyes became plaintive. "That was those other boys. They put him up to those things. Jimmy is a troubled boy—he's very sensitive, he never got over his father leaving—but he's not like those kids he runs around with. They put those ideas in his head. He never talked about dropping out until he met those boys, always on the street, always in trouble. A boy like Jimmy needs a man to look up to, to be an example."

"I'm sure you've heard that the rabbi was murdered Monday night," Orlando said.

"Jimmy wasn't here. He was in Puerto Rico. With family."

"We can check that out. What flight did he take? What's the name and address of the people he's staying with?"

Mrs. Rodriguez stood and set the tray on the table. "Just a minute, Mama." Her face glazed with anxiety, her mouth tight. "I'll get their address for you."

She left the room, and Briggs rose and began to pace. He took heavy steps, back and forth, the floor wincing beneath his feet. He stopped abruptly in front of a cluster of framed photographs on an end table.

"Fuck! I knew it!" He strode to one of the tall windows, threw it open, and stuck his head out. "Just what I thought! He's gone." He grabbed a picture from the table and thrust it at Orlando. "That lying bitch. That punk on the stairs was Jimmy Rodriguez. Look!"

Orlando stared into the smiling face of the boy they had seen on the steps.

Mrs. Rodriguez stood in the doorway with a slip of paper in her hand. "I have the address."

"Don't bother." Briggs pushed her aside and stormed down the hall toward the bedrooms.

"You can't go in there!" Mrs. Rodriguez cried. "That was another boy you saw. A neighbor boy. Jimmy is in Puerto Rico. He is!"

Orlando handed her the picture. "It's not very smart to lie to the police, Mrs. Rodriguez. If Jimmy has nothing to hide, why the games?" He heard a thunk and a crash, and went down the hall.

Briggs was taking the far bedroom apart. A mattress was thrown aside. A shelf above the bed was empty, books strewn on the floor. Drawers were open, contents tossed on the carpet. Briggs was bent over, rummaging in the closet.

"What are you doing?" Orlando's voice was taut.

"What does it look like?" Briggs flung a shoe aside.

"Briggs, you don't have a warrant."

Briggs pulled a cloth bag from a boot. Metal clinked inside. He dumped the contents out. A lock pick and a torsion wrench tumbled to the floor. "What do you call this?" Briggs scowled.

"Inadmissible evidence," Orlando said.

CHAPTER 9

Orlando stood alone on the corner of Seventy-second and Madison. Briggs had gone off to get a belated search warrant to dust for fingerprints in Jimmy Rodriguez's bedroom. Orlando didn't think it would come to much. Since the razor at the murder scene had no fingerprints, the perpetrator had probably used gloves. He doubted they would find any prints in the Rabowitz house that matched the ones in the boy's bedroom. Briggs had insisted the case was over, and an APB was put out for Rodriguez's arrest. At least this had the benefit of getting Briggs off his back for a while.

But Orlando wasn't so sure everything fit into place. Loose ties bothered him. A boy caught in the act of burglary might kill. But why the shaving? He fingered the copies of sales receipts in his pocket that he had taken from Rabowitz's rolltop desk.

The antique shop was small but elegant, the front window made up of tiny panes that showcased beautifully upholstered Louis XIV chairs. A smattering of the panes, reflecting the afternoon sun, had the hard shine of new glass. The others rippled with the waves of old glass, and probably dated from when the building was first erected in the early part of the century. Orlando stepped through the doorway to the tinkle of a bell above him. A spring closed the door with a bang.

A young Asian man appeared in a doorway in the back. The tightness of his expression showed he didn't approve of slamming doors or those responsible for them. He approached with swift feline movements. "May I help you?"

The shop was bigger than Orlando originally thought, and careful positioning of each piece of furniture allowed a surprising number of objects in the room. Orlando smelled incense. The gentle sound of classical music softened the room.

"I'd like to speak to the owner. Michael Serrout."

"Michel," the young man corrected, using the French pronunciation. "He's in back. If you'll follow me?" He turned on his heel and moved with gestures so smooth, Orlando wondered if he had been trained as a dancer. They threaded their way around chairs and tables. A vanity caught his eye, and Orlando stopped and rubbed his hand on the shiny surface.

"Beautiful marble," he murmured. It looked expensive.

"That's malachite."

Orlando pulled the price tag. Seven thousand dollars. Beautiful *and* expensive.

They passed through an office with a desk littered with papers and into a workroom. The heavy odor of lacquer overpowered despite an open back door. Furniture, not the same quality of the stuff out front, was stacked haphazardly in the corners. Newspapers were spread out on the floor, a fifties-style chair of green vinyl and blond wooden armrests at the center.

Michel Serrout looked up from a crouched position. Lacquer dripped from a brush in his hand. He looked to be in his forties, with dark hair and a pinched mustache that grew from narrow nostrils. He was stocky and muscular, with a tight shirt that said he was proud of his body.

"I like it," Orlando said, indicating the chair. "Very fifties. I didn't see this kind of thing in the shop."

Serrout was obviously pleased to talk about a subject he was interested in. "Up front everything is at least one hundred years old. Back here, I indulge myself. My penchant is fifties deco." His eyes sparkled. The accent was French. His chest puffed with pride. "I've been searching for this piece for years. It's a match with two I already have in my living room. I won't tell you what I had to pay to get it."

"So you do your own refinishing back here?"

"Only personal stuff. The rest is done professionally. This is just a little hobby of mine, remnants of my younger days when I first started out in this business, buying junky things and fixing them up and calling them antiques. Did you see something up front you were interested in?"

Orlando stepped forward and showed his badge.

"You were acquainted with Rabbi Avraham Rabowitz?"

The face fell, a net of wrinkles deepening under the eyes. Orlando saw that the hair was dyed. The antique dealer was well into his fifties. "He was a client. So sorry to hear of his death. Such a terrible thing." The brush dripped again, and Serrout laid it on an open can of Varathane. "Lee, why don't you take care of the front shop?" The young man slipped out of the room. Serrout's hazel eyes watched him go with the appreciation of a man observing a work of art.

Orlando pulled the receipts out of his pocket. "Can you explain these?"

"Why, yes. I sold some articles for Avraham Rabowitz. Generally I buy from people, then sell the things in my shop." He smiled. "At a greatly increased price. In this particular case, however, I served as a go-between between the buyers and the rabbi. For a fee, of course."

"And why is that?"

"Because I have contacts. Someone like Rabowitz wouldn't know people willing to buy the things he wanted to sell."

"That's not what I mean. Why not just sell the stuff directly to you?"

Serrout rose and wiped his hands on a rag. "That's the way Rabbi Rabowitz insisted it be done. He wanted to know who the buyer was before the sale went through. He reserved the right to reject any potential buyer."

"Is that usual?"

Serrout pursed his lips and shook his head. "I've been in this business thirty-fi—twenty-five years, and never once have I done this before."

"How long had this been going on?"

"More than a year. It was of great importance to the rabbi that the articles not appear on the market all at once. Discretion was paramount. He insisted on extreme caution, as these articles were of a . . ."—he searched for the word carefully, but not because of a lack of fluency in English—"delicate nature, and publicity of their sale would have been . . . unfortunate. His main stipulation was that the articles not be sold to any religious organization or their agent. He demanded I check out the buyer before finalizing the sale."

"What kind of articles are we talking about?"

"Antiques."

"What kind of antiques?"

Serrout appeared uncomfortable. "Uh. They were of a religious nature. A Torah, hand lettered and painted, 1847. A Holy Ark with gold inlays, a candelabrum . . ." His voice trailed off.

"Sounds like the booty from a looted synagogue," Orlando said. "Did you ask him where he got the stuff?"

Serrout gulped. "No, that would have been indiscreet. But I recently found out. About a month ago, I received a phone call—at home in the middle of the night—I was told if I wanted to live long that I'd better stop dealing with Rabowitz. That he had taken sacred articles from their sect, and was selling them on the open market for spite."

"Black market goods?"

"Hardly," Serrout snapped. "He had proof of ownership for all the articles I sold for him. All reputable dealers insist on that."

"But you didn't stop. I have an uncashed check here dated last week."

Serrout sighed. "No, I didn't stop. The articles were so unusual and of such fine quality. Quality rarely seen in a shop this size. The kind of pieces that almost never come on the market. Dealing in goods like that brings a shop prestige."

"But I thought you sold these objects discreetly," Orlando said.

Serrout winked. "In this business, word gets around. Always."

"And you never heard from the night caller again?"

"Oh, yes, I heard from them again. You might say they left their calling card. They smashed my front window one night. Had it not been for the iron-barred gate I lock up the storefront with, they probably would have ruined the whole place. As it was, the most they could do was break a few panes in the front window through the bars. The next day, I spoke with the people who live above the shops along the street. They heard the crash and saw four Hasidic men speed off in a car." He gave a tight smile. "None of them bothered to telephone the police. They all assumed someone else must have called."

"Under the circumstances, especially after Rabowitz's murder, did you ever consider calling the police yourself, and telling them of the connection between this and the rabbi?"

The dealer seemed very tired. Bags hung from his eyes. "I have worked very hard to build a respectable business. To call the police and bring this all up, it would have been ... uh ..."

"Indiscreet?"

Serrout stared at the floor.

"What night was the window broken?"

"Monday night."

"The night of the murder," Orlando said.

Menachem Rabowitz opened the door a crack, his face expressionless, his eyes colorless and inscrutable behind thick lenses. He said nothing.

"I've got to talk with you, Rabowitz," Orlando said. His voice bordered on a growl.

"Yes?" He held the door tightly.

"Look," Orlando said, "you can let me in

and we can talk civilized, or I can drag your ass down to headquarters. Right now, I'm inclined to do the latter."

Menachem Rabowitz paled. "All right. Please come in." He unlocked the gate and motioned Orlando inside. A little boy was playing in the living room, his arms outstretched. His head, shaved close, carried a skull cap.

"Barrrooooom! Daddy, I'm flying," he cried. "Come watch me."

"Later, Asher," Menachem Rabowitz said. "I'll come play later." To Orlando: "We can talk in the study."

The little boy registered disappointment, then went on with his game.

They passed the kitchen. The woman in the wig Orlando had seen the morning before was still there. She was preparing a pie, rolling out dough on a cutting board. A brown-haired girl, all curls, sat on a tall stool at her mother's side, watching. The woman looked up at them, then quickly back to her crust. Her eyes were troubled. Orlando wondered what she could tell him.

The study was lined with books from floor to ceiling, the only relief a barred window looking out on the backyard. A tricycle lay overturned on the patio. Menachem Rabowitz took a seat behind an oak desk and motioned Orlando to an easy chair in the corner.

"What can I do for you today?" He clasped his hands on top of the desk. Nervously.

Orlando eased into the chair and found himself sinking deeply into its cushions. "You can start by telling me the circumstances surrounding your brother's departure from your sect, keeping in mind that lying to a police officer is a crime."

Menachem Rabowitz leaned back in his chair and said in a steady, clearly enunciated cadence, as if talking to a slow child, "My brother left our sect nearly two years ago, shortly after the death of our father. I have not associated with him since."

"Did he take anything with him?"

"Like what?"

"Like a Torah, hand letter and painted, 1847. Like a Holy Ark with gold inlays."

Menachem Rabowitz sat up in his chair, his fingers toying with the blotter on the desk. "He may have."

Orlando leaned forward, gripping supple armrests. "I've already spoken with the antique dealer, Michel Serrout. I know your brother was selling religious articles, and it doesn't take a genius to figure out they came from your synagogue. Now tell me the truth, or we'll continue this discussion at police headquarters under a very bright spotlight."

Menachem Rabowitz gave him a poker face, eyes impenetrable.

Orlando shook his head. "You're stupid, you know that? There are witnesses to a group of Hasids trashing Serrout's front window. You seem to forget that people live above those shops. And when a gang of Hasidic Jews in traditional garb jump out of a car and smash a window, it gets noticed."

"Lies!" Menachem Rabowitz spit out, arms folded tightly under his chest.

"That the antiques came from your synagogue or that you were wearing traditional garb?"

"I deny all your accusations, which are merely conjecture. I suggest you get some proof before you bust in here next time with your lies." He pushed himself up from the chair and leaned over the desk, hands pressing firmly on the desktop. "Now get out." For the first time, Orlando saw his teeth, which were narrow and white.

"Sit down," Orlando ordered.

Menachem Rabowitz stood his ground.

Orlando shrugged. "I'd hate for your wife and kids to know that I'm going to throw you in the can with a bunch of pimps and crackhead throat cutters. If you don't care for your neighborhood, wait until you see the lovely jail cell I have waiting for you."

Menachem Rabowitz slowly sank back into his seat. "Okay." He sighed. "I'll tell you what you want to know. First, I have done nothing illegal. I know nothing of the violence you have mentioned. I do know about the religious articles."

"I'm waiting. Skeptically."

Menachem Rabowitz cleared his throat, as if to begin a long story. "The eldest son in every generation in my family becomes a rabbi. It was true of my brother, our father, our grandfather, going back several generations. There were certain articles that were passed down from generation to generation. The Torah, the Holy Ark, a number of others. They were legally the property of my family, and always left to the eldest son, but morally they belong to the synagogue. They were used in our services since as far back as the very eldest of our members can remember. They were part of our lives, sacred."

Menachem Rabowitz took off his glasses and rubbed his eyes. They were pale blue and held great sadness.

"After my father died, they became the property of my brother, following both tradition and my father's will."

"What did you get?"

"My father's diamond business."

"I'll bet your brother was happy about that."

"I deserved it. I've put my heart and soul in that business all my life. Avraham was already well-off with his real estate holdings. And my father wouldn't have left him anything if he knew Avraham was going to abandon us. When he told me he was leaving us, I begged him to stay. He was my brother and I loved him. It never occurred to me that he would even consider taking the Torah and the rest of the things. When he carted them off, I told him his crime amounted to killing his own father. He just laughed at me, and said my kind

would be the end of this world because we did
nothing to stop the decay ravaging our society.

"We offered to buy them from him, but he
told us he'd rather dump them in a ditch than
sell them to us. He told me he was going to
sell them, one by one, on the open market. He
said he'd sell only to collectors interested in
their historical value. That things sacred to
us would sit in some collector's study, to be
observed like a cell under a microscope or in
some museum to be gawked at and then forgotten. I realized then that Avraham hated us all,
my father, me, our lives, our beliefs. He
thought we were weak. This was his way of
telling us we could go to Hell."

"So you tracked down the articles to a little
shop on Seventy-second and Madison, and you
decided to get revenge."

"No," Menachem Rabowitz said. "We took
the legal route. We got a restraining order to
stop Avraham from selling anything and went
to court. But we lost the case—the court ruled
in Avraham's favor—and that was it. I never
saw or spoke to my brother again, and considered the case closed."

Orlando frowned, shook his head, and sighed.

"Believe what you will," Menachem Rabowitz said, "but I'm telling the truth. Check it
out with anyone from our synagogue. We
were devastated by what Avraham did, but to
commit acts of violence over it would have
been ..."—he searched for the right word—
"... sacrilegious." He bent forward and asked

in a near whisper, "Why are you trying to hang this on me? I'm a law-abiding citizen. I was here with my wife all Monday night."

Orlando rose. "We'll see about that. I'll let myself out." He closed the study door behind him and went down the hall. He stopped at the kitchen doorway. The woman was laying the dough in a pie plate. She looked up, then bent and whispered to the little girl. The girl gave Orlando a frightened look, jumped from the stool, and went out the back door.

"I'd like to talk to you," Orlando said. "About Monday night. Was your husband here the entire evening?"

She set the pie plate aside and nodded. "He was home from work by six." Her brown eyes were gentle, her features soft and pretty. She wore an apron over her long-sleeved blue dress. "I shouldn't be speaking with you alone. You must leave."

But Orlando sensed she wanted to talk.

"It's better if you tell the truth," Orlando said. "I'm already aware of the things Avraham Rabowitz took from your synagogue."

She looked startled, then relaxed a little, but a wariness remained. "So you know," she said. "I'm glad." She crossed the kitchen and adjusted the temperature of the oven. "Then maybe you can understand why Menachem seems so ... hard. He isn't really. He's a wonderful husband, and he's crazy about our kids. But Avraham hurt us so deeply, not just our family, but the whole synagogue." She returned to the counter and worked on the pie, glancing up at Orlando occasionally. "Our lives haven't been the same since. You see, Menachem loved his brother dearly, worshiped him. Love like that turns bitter when one is betrayed."

Orlando could tell she was uncomfortable having him there, but he didn't go. "You know," he said, "I've spent my whole life in Brooklyn, but I don't know anything about your culture. I see Hasidic men on the subway train or sometimes on the street, but I don't think I've ever spoken to one till this case. It doesn't make it easy to find Avraham Rabowitz's killer."

She finished with the pie and wiped her hands on a towel. She looked him directly in the eye, then averted her gaze. "You find us difficult to understand, don't you?"

Orlando was taken aback by her bluntness.

She smiled. "You don't have to answer, I can see. I know the preconceptions. That we're rigid and narrow. That we never bathe and have a dozen children. That we Hasidic women are shy and passive. I hear what people say." She gave him an ironic look. "They have a tendency to speak loudly enough to be overheard. Don't you see what a relief it is for us to have our own stores, our own community, where we can be comfortable and treated with respect?"

Orlando nodded. He thought of gays who preferred living in gay neighborhoods.

"We have something special here. Something sacred." She glanced out the window at her children playing in the yard. "We have great schools where our children really learn. And not just the history they teach in public schools, but *our* history. And they learn about faith. The faith that has preserved us through thousands of years of persecution."

She took the pie to the oven and put it in. "I know even secular Jews sometimes laugh at us, as if we're distant cousins that are an embarrassment to the family. I wish they could see how we really live. We've built a world where faith in God brings meaning to our lives, where raising children is a gift from God. With so many people in this world drifting and unhappy, why does it bother people that we have found a path that fulfills us?" Suddenly, she was looking beyond Orlando, and her eyes widened. Orlando spun around. Menachem Rabowitz stood in the hallway.

"The front door is that way." Menachem Rabowitz said, pointing down the hall.

Orlando strolled through the residential section of Williamsburg. The peacefulness, disturbed only by the hum of car engines in the distance, settled into him. He recalled the severity of Menachem Rabowitz's expression upon finding Orlando alone with his wife. He had a feeling Menachem hadn't been upset by what his wife might have told him, but that he'd been offended the detective had spoken to her without a member of the community present. Well, it wasn't the first time Orlando had made a mistake when dealing with the diverse cultures he knew so little about in this city. It went with the job.

He crossed a silent street, its blacktop blemished with potholes from the tough months of winter. A man in a black hat and coat stood in the middle of the block before a brownstone that had been converted into a synagogue. He grasped a can in one hand and an old brush in the other, and daubed paint on the front of the building.

As Orlando approached, the man turned, his earlocks jumping into motion then settling at the sides of his strong face. He was young, about twenty, and his thin beard looked soft to the touch. He wasn't painting the whole brownstone, just a series of splotches along the front at eye level.

"Vandalism?"

The young man nodded. "I always like to get it covered as soon as possible. The older people on the block, I don't like them to see it. Not the ones who survived the holocaust. It's too painful. The younger ones, now them I want to see it. I want them to know. It's important they see it can happen even in this neighborhood. Anyway, whenever you see paint spots on a synagogue, you know what it's covering up."

"You called the police?"

"Yes. Sometimes they catch them. But there

are always more to take their place." His voice was a rich baritone, but he spoke quietly, as if he knew its power and chose to use it carefully. "Are you a cop?"

"You can tell?"

"Strangers don't come around here a lot, and there have been a number of police around because of the Rabowitz murder. After a while you kind of sense it." He gave Orlando an apologetic grin.

"You hear of anybody who saw anything?"

He shook his head. "It happened three blocks from here. But everyone's feeling the effects." He waited to see if Orlando understood what he meant.

Orlando did. "You're not planning on joining that neighborhood patrol, are you?"

The young man scoffed. "You kidding? Those nuts are trying to make this a racial thing, but where's the evidence? You know, other than a few Rambos on both sides, the different groups in this neighborhood get along pretty well. I wish those hotheads would just shut up."

"You ever meet Rabowitz?"

He shook his head. "I was lucky enough to avoid that dubious honor. He was always ranting about something, saying inflammatory things. I have a feeling we wouldn't have seen eye to eye." The young man finished his job and set the can and brush down. "That's the terrible thing about keeping to yourself. Everyone misunderstands you, and assumes the loudest of your members represent the whole." He paused thoughtfully, then asked the detective, "How can the police solve this murder when you know nothing of us?"

Orlando didn't have an answer.

A tall thin old man with a great beard of white curls came down the street, his cane *click-clicking* against the sidewalk. The young man watched him approach, turned to Orlando. "I have to go in for a minute, but could you wait for me?" He helped the old man up the stairs to the double doors of the synagogue, gently holding his elder's arm as they climbed.

Orlando waited a minute, and the young man returned with a big book in his hand. "This is for you," he said. "It will tell you about us." He grinned. "Don't worry, it looks more imposing than it is. It's a good start for understanding who we are. When you're done, come back and we'll talk."

Orlando took the book and thanked him. They introduced themselves. "Do you work here?" Orlando asked.

"I hope to." He grinned again. "I'm in college now. I want to be a rabbi."

Orlando nodded and smiled back. "I'm sure you'll be a good one." He watched the young man pick up the paint can and brush, and disappear into the synagogue.

CHAPTER 10

Orlando found a parking spot in front of the Greenbergs' brownstone. Michael Greenberg's Mercedes was nowhere to be seen. Dusk was approaching, and a cool ribbon of orange colored the horizon. The gentle breeze of the afternoon had gone sharp and brittle. Orlando slipped from behind the wheel and took the stairs slowly. It had been a long day. He felt his head. The knot was still there. He pushed the bell and heard a melody chime inside the apartment. A woman in her thirties opened the door. She stared at him, wiping her hands with a dish towel. Orlando introduced himself.

She nodded. "I saw you out the window this morning speaking with my husband. How do you do? I'm Anna Greenberg." She reached out a damp hand. "Oh, sorry." She laughed. "I'm doing dishes." When she laughed, her brown eyes sparkled. Her hair was a rich auburn and bounced in lively waves when she moved. She seemed years younger, in age and in manner, than her sister. "Michael is running an errand for me, but he should be back in a minute."

"Actually, I hoped to speak with Mrs. Rabowitz."

"Oh. Well, she's sleeping. Michael has been keeping her sedated. This has been a terrible shock for Sarah. But why don't you come in and wait in the living room? Michael will be back soon."

"I'll help you dry," Orlando offered. It was a chance to find out if Anna knew anything about the murder.

She flashed him a smile, took his coat, and hung it in the closet, then handed him the damp towel. "By all means, be my guest."

They passed a girl of about ten sitting at the dining room table, school books and papers spread out around her. "Mom, I don't get this math stuff." She leaned her elbows on the table and hung her face on her fists.

"You'll have to wait until Dad gets home, dear. He's the genius in the family." She pushed open the swinging kitchen door and turned back to Orlando. "I majored in art in college. Painting, pottery, that's my style. When the kids have questions about figures, I send them to their father."

The kitchen was small and old-fashioned, with a big white sink and painted cupboards. The refrigerator and range, matching bronze and in the latest style, seemed out of place.

"You'd think a doctor's wife wouldn't have to hover over a sink, but we don't have room in here for a dishwasher. So much for the myth that these old houses have big kitchens.

We hope to tear out a wall to make a little more room."

She stood over a sink full of suds. "Oh, how rude of me. Let me offer you something to drink. Coffee? You can sip while you dry." She poured a cup and set it on the counter by the dish rack. Her hands disappeared into the suds.

"You don't seem much like your sister," Orlando said.

"Really? Well, Sarah always was very serious. She was the baby of the family."

"I would have thought you were younger."

Anna shook her head and handed him a dripping pot. "No, I'm the eldest. There's two years difference. I'm afraid Sarah's had a hard life."

Orlando wiped the pot with a towel, then looked helpless.

"Right lower cupboard," she said.

Orlando opened the cupboard and set the pot inside. "I take it your family is not Hasidic."

"Heavens no. All that tradition and ritual would stifle me to death. I hate that. I'm not going to have any church or synagogue tell me how to live. No thanks."

"You and your sister weren't raised that way?"

Anna found a scouring pad under the sink and wrestled with a particularly tough spot. "We were raised Jewish, but not Hasidic. Good grief no. My family was part of that whole Jewish-leftist-radical thing in the thirties. My grandfather was a Lincoln Brigader. Don't get me wrong. I consider myself religious, but I'm not *that* religious. No, that's not the way Sarah was raised."

"What happened?"

Anna shrugged. "She met Avraham. She fell in love. She converted. It's not an interesting story." She handed him a plate.

"You didn't approve."

"It's not that I didn't approve. It's just not my idea of a fun life. I know the lifestyle they live brings a lot of joy and meaning to their lives, but it's not for me. I don't want to hide away in Williamsburg, and never meet anybody but my own kind. That's too small a world for me."

"Tell me what happened Monday night."

Anna gazed at him appraisingly. "Sarah and the kids came over at, oh, I don't know, maybe nine o'clock. We just sat around the dining room table gabbing. I can't even remember what we talked about. The kids were playing downstairs. We lost track of the time, and the kids fell asleep in the playroom. They sleep over here all the time anyway, so we just put them to bed. Sarah left at twelve-fifteen. Then we got a call after two in the morning, with Sarah crying on the phone that Avraham had been murdered. I guess you know the rest."

"If I knew the rest, I wouldn't be here." Orlando put a plate on a cupboard shelf. "What do you know about the feud between the rabbi and his brother Menachem?"

"I know there was bad blood between them. Their father left Menachem the diamond business, and Avraham got some synagogue trinkets."

"I spoke with Menachem Rabowitz today. They don't consider those things trinkets."

Anna pulled the plug and the drain slurped. "I didn't mean to be flip. Anyway, Avraham left in a storm of bad feelings. You have to understand that their whole family is so extreme. Everything is a life-and-death issue with them. When Avraham took those things, the sect went crazy. Sarah begged him to give them back. She was scared for her life. And for the children."

"You think they might have killed him?"

Anna borrowed the towel and wiped her hands. "I don't know. I hate to think it, but it's possible." She hung the towel on the refrigerator door handle. "Let's sit in the living room. Bring your coffee." She poured herself a cup.

The living room was expensively furnished, with darkly stained hardwood floors and plushly cushioned couches. Orlando sank into one and put his cup on a plate-glass coffee table in front of him. Anna sat in an armchair. She held a saucer and sipped the coffee. A heavy antique clock hung on the wall behind her and ticked solemnly.

"You know what's bothering me?" Orlando leaned forward, hands resting on his knees. "Hasidic men don't shave. Rabowitz had a beard. What was he doing with that shaving kit on the dresser?"

Anna choked on her drink. "You didn't know? Oh, of course, you haven't been able to speak with Sarah. Someone sent Avraham that shaving kit. He got it in the mail, oh, a week or so ago. Sarah mentioned it to me. She didn't have any idea who it was from. There was no return address. All I know is, Avraham was very upset about it but wouldn't say why."

It was Orlando's turn to choke on his coffee. "Why weren't we told this before? I've got to talk with Mrs. Rabowitz. *Now*." He stood.

Tiny frown lines creased the corners of Anna's mouth. "I can't let you do that. Michael said she can't be disturbed." She set her cup in its saucer with finality.

"I'm already up." Mrs. Rabowitz stood in the doorway to the living room, leaning against the door frame. She appeared even smaller than when Orlando had first seen her, a wisp of a woman. Her short hair stuck to her head, her face pale, haunted. A thick brown blanket was draped over her shoulders, held tightly around her neck by frail hands. The blanket cascaded down to thick slippers, then formed a train behind her.

"Sarah! You shouldn't be up. You know what Michael said." Anna put her cup and saucer on a table. She rose and went to Mrs. Rabowitz's side. "You need your rest, dear." She took her sister's elbow and steered her to the armchair. Mrs. Rabowitz eased herself into the cushions with the lack of agility of an old woman. Anna perched on the armrest, her hand gently massaging her sister's back.

"What do you want to know, Officer ..." her voice drifted off.

"Orlando. Remember, we met Monday night."

"Yes, Detective Orlando. Now I remember."

Mrs. Rabowitz's pupils were big black pools. *What was Michael Greenberg shooting into her?* Whatever the stuff was, it was doping her to oblivion. Why?

Orlando straightened. "I need you to answer some questions, if you can. Your husband received a razor anonymously in the mail last week, the same razor used to cut his throat. Tell me the details."

Her eyes seemed to focus on the cup in Orlando's hand. "It came in a brown paper package marked personal. I set it on the dining room table for him when he got home that evening. When he took it out of the package, he turned white."

"Did you keep the package? We could dust for fingerprints."

"Oh, no. Avraham threw it out. He didn't say another word about it. But he was silent for the rest of the evening. He seemed frightened."

Orlando frowned and nodded. "Mrs. Rabowitz, I found a number of land-option agreements in your husband's desk. Your husband was optioning land in Williamsburg worth hundreds of millions of dollars."

Mrs. Rabowitz blinked. "Hundreds of millions of dollars?" she said helplessly. "Where would we get hundreds of millions of dollars?"

"I was hoping you could tell me."

"We have some apartment buildings. That's all." Her eyes wandered, confused. "Hundreds of millions of dollars?"

"Avraham was a typical Hasid," Anna put in, stroking her sister's lank hair. "He was the man, he took care of business. Sarah wouldn't know that kind of thing."

Orlando paced the floor, his heels clacking on the waxed hardwood. Outside the row of front windows, darkness had fallen. Streetlights cast soft light on the stark trees lining the sidewalk.

"I visited your place last night. I heard something in one of the back bedrooms. When I went to investigate, someone bashed me over the head with a hard object. You have any idea of who it might have been?"

Mrs. Rabowitz's eyes widened. "Last night? My house?" Her hands pulled the blanket tighter around her neck.

"Whoever it was, he was ransacking your son's bedroom."

Mrs. Rabowitz let out a gasp, and Anna set firm supportive hands on her sister's shoulders. Anna threw a hard look of reproach at him. Steel features said she didn't want her sister disturbed.

"I'm sorry if I'm upsetting you, Mrs. Rabowitz," Orlando said, stopping in mid-stride. "But I've got to have answers if I'm going to apprehend your husband's killer. I know about the rabbi's split from his brother's sect and the ensuing bad feelings. Could Menachem Rabowitz or someone else in his sect have broken into your house in an attempt to get those religious articles back?"

Mrs. Rabowitz shook her head weakly. "Avraham never kept those things at home. They were kept in safety deposit vaults until they were sold. Menachem must know that."

"You never know," Anna said. "Those people were frantic when Avraham took those things. I honestly wouldn't put anything past them."

Mrs. Rabowitz buried her face in the folds of the blanket. "Oh," she sobbed, "why didn't Avraham just give those things back?"

Anna wrapped her arms around Mrs. Rabowitz and rocked her gently back and forth. She looked up at Orlando admonishingly. "Didn't I tell you this would happen?" Then to her sister: "It's all right, dear. Everything will be all right."

The front door burst open, and Michael Greenberg stood in the doorway holding a bag of groceries. An icy breeze blew in with him. A deep frown lined his face, his fat cheeks smudged with color. He pushed the door closed behind him. "What's going on here? Sarah should be in bed."

Anna looked up from her huddled position. "New York's finest had questions to ask." She shot Orlando a savage glance.

Greenberg surveyed Orlando. "I guess I should have known. Don't you understand that Sarah is a very sick woman? What more can she possibly tell you about the murder? Go after Avraham's enemies, not his family. We've suffered enough."

"I can't find the killer if I don't have all the facts. Rabowitz was murdered two nights ago, and I just now learn that the razor used to slash his throat was sent to him anonymously last week."

Greenberg blanched. "I wouldn't know about that."

The little girl Orlando had seen earlier scampered into the room. She clung to her father's coat. "Daddy, is Aunt Sarah going to be all right?"

He set the bag of groceries on the floor and ran his fingers through her brown curls. "Yes, dear. She just needs rest. Now why don't you go to your room? I'll come up in a bit."

"I need help on my math," the girl whined.

"Later, honey. Just go to your room now."

The girl regarded him doubtfully, then slipped out of the arched doorway of the living room without a sound.

"Now I want you back in bed," he said to Mrs. Rabowitz. Anna helped her up from the chair and led her from the room.

Greenberg unzipped his coat. "I don't mind answering any questions you might have, but please remember, I'm Sarah's doctor and I say she's not well enough to talk to the police."

"I think she would be if she wasn't so spaced out on drugs. Why are you giving her so much?"

The doctor's face went tight. "After what you just witnessed, I should think the answer would be perfectly clear."

"Mrs. Rabowitz cried. That's a natural response to what has happened. You don't cover grief with drugs."

"Is that your expert opinion as a physician?"

"It's my opinion as a human being."

Greenberg sighed. "I'm sorry, I didn't mean to take it out on you. It's just that there's been a tremendous amount of pressure on us since Avraham was murdered, what with reporters calling and all the sensationalism in the tabloids." He gave a sheepish smile. "You can't blame a guy for losing his cool. Was Sarah able to help you?"

Orlando shrugged. "Maybe. Too many pieces still don't fit." Some of the details of the murder had already been leaked to the press—headlines screamed about the prayer shawl stuffed in Rabowitz's mouth—though no mention yet of the shaving.

Greenberg got Orlando his coat and walked him to his car. A steady wind gusted down the narrow canyon of the street. Orlando lifted his collar. Lights were on in most of the brownstones now, and the street was deserted of people except the occasional businessman arriving home from the office. Greenberg stood at the car door as Orlando got in.

"Did you check out the Rodriguez boy?"

Orlando nodded. "Yeah, we have an APB out on him. He'll turn up."

"You don't sound like you think he did it."

Orlando turned the ignition. "I think this murder is a lot more complex than a punk kid getting revenge on a boss who fired him." The car sputtered to life.

Greenberg looked thoughtful, then said, "Well, if you have any more questions . . ."

"I do. Do you know if anyone else has a key to the Rabowitz home? Say, a neighbor? Did the Rabowitzes leave a key with anyone when they went on vacation?"

"I thought you people said the killer probably used burglary tools."

"The night of the murder. Someone was there last night."

"I don't know. They may have left a key with the people next door in case of emergency. You suspect the killer returned to the house last night?"

Orlando shut the car door and rolled down the window. "Yeah, and I've got a knot the size of a golf ball on top of my head to prove it."

Orlando turned the volume low so as not to disturb Stewart, then settled onto the couch to watch the eleven-o'clock news. He glanced over at his other half, who groaned wearily and scribbled something in the margin of the exam in his lap, then flipped the page. They hadn't said much to each other since the night before, and Orlando had softened the severity of the silence between them by playing Horowitz on the compact disc player most of the evening.

They had eaten a late dinner of Chinese takeout, then Stewart went back to his exams and Orlando picked up the book the young man at the synagogue had given him. The author, a Jewish woman, had spent a year living among the Hasidim, and the book detailed her experiences and the tenets of their culture. Orlando had read the introduction, then, exhausted from the long day, laid the book aside in favor of the evening news.

Poindexter rose from his basket in the corner, pattered over to the couch, and stuck his nose in Orlando's crotch. "How rude!" Orlando exclaimed with mock indignation, looking up to catch his lover's reaction. "At least someone still shows an interest in me." But Stewart remained lost in the test on his lap. Pushing the dog away, Orlando sighed and took a sip from the mug on the coffee table. His decaf was laced with rum. At first he had feared Stewart would smell it on his breath, but considering how things were going, what chance was there of that?

Bleakly, he glanced at the television screen. The top news story made him jump to attention.

"The home of a Williamsburg woman was firebombed tonight, an incident sure to escalate tensions between blacks and Hasidic Jews in the Brooklyn neighborhood," the blond newswoman said. "Jewel Jefferson, a black woman, was putting her children to bed at eight-thirty this evening when she smelled smoke. As she rushed her three children and her aging mother from the house, they heard someone chanting, "Burn, burn, burn." According to police, a witness saw three young men, one dressed in a black coat and fedora, the other two in blue coats, run from behind Mrs. Jefferson's house to a dormitory for Hasidic Jews at a nearby yeshiva."

Cut to an administrator at the yeshiva: "Rumors that the murderer of Rabbi Avraham Rabowitz was black may have led to this tragic incident. The young men here are good and decent. I can't believe that any of them would be involved in such a thing, but we'll cooperate with the police in every way we can to get to the bottom of this."

Cut to the blond anchor: "Police say someone placed a cardboard box with a can of petroleum inside in Mrs. Jefferson's basement and set it ablaze. While no serious damage was done to the house, residents worry that the incident may incite retaliatory acts from the black community."

Cut to a portly man with yarmulke: "This is a terrible thing, but if the media blows it all out of proportion, we could see a lot of violence. If some Hasidic kids did do this, *they* should be punished, not the whole community."

Cut to anchor: "But the controversial black activist Reverend Melvin Packard disagrees."

Cut to Packard: "Young people don't commit acts of violence out of the blue. The baseball-bat attack against blacks in Howard Beach did not occur in a vacuum. The shooting of Yusef Hawkins by a gang of Italian youths in Bensonhurst did not just happen. And children don't firebomb the homes of their neighbors unless they're taught to. This is learned behavior, learned from parents, schools, religion, the media. And the Jews of Williamsburg have sent a signal to their children by forming that vigilante squad, a so-called neighborhood patrol that excludes blacks: it's open season on the black community."

Cut to anchor: "The Reverend Packard vows to flood the neighborhood with black protesters if the neighborhood patrol is not disbanded. Meanwhile, no arrests have been made in the firebombing."

Orlando put his hand to his mouth and muttered. "Just what I needed." His worst fears about the case were coming true. A murder, pure and simple, was being twisted into a media event to be exploited by all sides for their own gain.

Stewart, looking up from his test, eyed Orlando with concern. "What's this going to do to your case?"

Shaking his head, Orlando said glumly, "Make it twice as hard to find Rabowitz's killer. All this hostility and finger pointing is just going to cloud what really happened." He was lucky it was still winter. Under the oppressive heat of summer, Williamsburg would have been in flames by now.

"Isn't that Reverend Packard the one that protested at the grand jury probe of Briggs?"

Orlando nodded. "Yeah. And he was there at Howard Beach and in Bensonhurst with his followers, protesting. I'm sympathetic with his cause, but not his tactics. The guy is only interested in inflaming passions."

"That, and drawing attention to himself. He's so angry, he can't see straight."

Anger like that could spread like fire and leave everyone burned. "The only thing that's going to calm things down is solving this murder."

"Unless, of course, the killer was black," Stewart said, looking back to the exam. "Then we're in for a long hot summer."

Orlando woke in darkness, reached over, and wrapped his arms around Stewart. His lover's breathing was slow, shallow, but his body was too rigid to be asleep.

"You awake?" Orlando whispered.

Silence. Then, "Yes, I'm awake."

"Got the exams on your mind?"

Stewart sighed, pulled away. "Doug, we've got to talk. We haven't, you know, for a long time."

Orlando propped his head on his hand,

elbow cushioned by the pillow. "You're the one who's so busy with your exams."

"That's one week per session. And you're talking about sex. I'm talking about communication." Stewart stroked Orlando's hair. "I know you've started drinking, not a lot, but some. I've been afraid if I say something, it'll just make the problem worse. I don't know what to do, I just feel you drifting away from me. You talk of trivial things, but you never tell me how you really feel."

"That's because you don't want to hear it," Orlando said quietly.

Stewart gripped Orlando's hand. "I do! I love you. You think I don't want to know when someone bashes you on the head? Why would you try to hide a thing like that from me? I don't understand why you're shutting me out."

Orlando felt his temperature rise. "Because you *don't* want to hear it. Every time I share something with you, you harp about me quitting my job. And I'm not going to do that, Stewart, I'm not. I don't have a good reason, I don't have to. This is what I am. I just wouldn't be me anymore without what I do on the force. And I'm not going to stop being me for you, for Ma, or for some bigots in the department."

"I want to help you, I want to be included in your life. But don't expect me to feel good about you being partners with Briggs." Stewart paused. "I'm only saying what any lover would. That I'm afraid for you working in a place like that. That I'm afraid of what it's doing to us."

They were silent for a minute, then Orlando said, "You've always trusted my judgment in the past. Believe in me now. I need you to support me in my work, no matter how you feel about it."

Stewart let out a deep breath, then flipped on his side, away from Orlando, and hugged a pillow. He was quiet for a long time. Finally, he said, "Okay, I'll make you a deal. You stop cutting me out of your life, and I'll keep my mouth shut about your job. Deal?"

An uneasy truce if there ever was one.

Orlando moved over and held Stewart in his arms.

"Deal," he said.

CHAPTER 11

Orlando lay awake, gazing at the spears of early morning light slanting down through the partially closed venetian blinds. It was chilly, and he pulled the comforter up and held its thick folds tightly around his neck. Stewart curled beside him, clutching a fat pillow, snoring. Orlando had not been awakened by the snores: they didn't bother him. A gentle nudge in the ribs would cure that problem. No, it was Gus, that stupid dog from next door. The retriever had howled at the moon half the night, and was now greeting the rising sun with a frenzy of barks usually reserved for the mailman. Stuffing his head between pillows hadn't obliterated the sound, and Orlando found it impossible to sleep like that anyway. He sighed and decided to give up.

He slipped out of bed, careful not to wake Stewart, and wrapped himself in a maroon terry-cloth robe. His back ached, and he massaged the knot on his head. Smaller, but still there, tender to the touch. Stewart gave a quick snort, then softly wheezed in his sleep.

The floor was cold, and he searched under the bed for his slippers. He found them in a nest of dust balls.

Orlando didn't flip on the light switch in the kitchen. He wasn't ready for artificial light, not this early in the morning. He set the coffee brewing. The curtains above the sink were open, revealing a layer of fog that hung thickly over the neighborhood. Gus ran in circles in the neighbor's fenced backyard, apparently barking at his tail.

"Damn stupid dog," Orlando grumbled, reaching for a mug in the cupboard.

Neighbors on all sides had complained about the dog, to no avail. Stewart had once spied Gus's owner, a portly woman in a sweatshirt and tight pants, hanging up laundry in the backyard. Sticking his head out the window, he had asked her to keep the dog in at night, to which she had retorted, "Don't worry about it!" But nothing changed. Occasionally a frustrated neighbor was heard screaming, "Shut that fucking dog up! I can't even hear myself think in my own house!" Some looked to Orlando for help, but he was as powerless as the rest of them. In a city where murder records are broken every year, arresting someone for having a noisy pet would have brought laughter and contempt at the station house. And Orlando had enough of that already.

Rummaging through the refrigerator, he found a bagel and smeared it with cream cheese, put it on a plate, and settled at the table. The aroma of coffee was enough to clear the sleep from his head. Orlando sipped it, and steam rising from the mug tickled his nose. Warmth spread in his stomach. He felt good for the first time in a long time, right with the world. The coffee made him forget about the dog, and his problems at work seemed far away. He was thinking about Stewart, curled in bed, cozy under a soft comforter. Stewart, with his firm and finely muscled body, smooth skin, and sand-colored chest hair. Stewart, with those blue eyes that drove Orlando crazy.

Orlando downed the bagel, swallowed the last drops of coffee, and pushed the chair back. He had no luck when they went to bed the night before, Stewart begging off with, "I'm so sleepy. After test week." Well, it was morning now, after a long night of rest. Orlando peered in the bedroom. Stewart had stopped snoring. The comforter lay in a heap on the floor. Stewart was on his stomach, hugging a pillow, legs spread. Only a sheet rippled over the contours of his body.

Orlando shed his robe and stood over the bed. Stewart breathed slowly, steadily. His body seemed to sway with each breath. Orlando pulled back the sheet in a leisurely fashion, unveiling a body white as a statue and as beautifully sculpted. He stared down, awed, then slipped into bed, his frame fitting perfectly the curving form beside him. He nibbled Stewart's long neck, cradled Stewart's face in his hands, and planted a firm kiss on inviting lips. Stewart opened his eyes. They looked gray in the dimness of the room.

"Go away, coffee breath."

Orlando sighed. No luck this morning either.

"You can't say you're too sleepy, not after a good night's rest," Orlando gently prodded.

Stewart stretched and yawned. "You crazy? That mongrel next door kept me awake half the night. Tell you what, you shoot that dog, and after test week, I'll have sex with you." He rolled over, hid his head under the pillow, and mumbled, "Besides, you know I don't like wild sex in the morning."

"English professors," Orlando muttered. "You can't live with 'em, you can't live without 'em." He gathered the comforter from the floor and spread it over Stewart, tucking it in around him. "Well, if you won't let me keep you warm, I guess this will have to do." He bent to pick up his robe.

"Thanks, big boy," Stewart mumbled drowsily into his pillow. In a moment he was asleep again.

In the kitchen, Orlando poured himself another mug of coffee, then wandered into the living room. He was too alert to go back to bed—and the temptations that waited there were too great—and it was too early to go to the station house. He set the mug on the book about Hasidic culture the young man at the synagogue had given him the day before. The university-press paperback sat forlornly on the coffee table, somehow out of place here, in the home of nonbelievers.

Orlando dropped into the armchair and switched on the lamp. Yellow brightness stung his eyes. He took a sip from the mug, set it aside, and brought the book to his lap. It lay there, ponderous, like a mystery unsolved. He flipped through its pages, stopping at sections that piqued his curiosity. It struck him that there were people who lived lives totally disparate from his, in worlds of their own with sins and punishments and justifications for each that he couldn't imagine. Traditions that seemed silly and unthinkable to him took on deadly importance in others' eyes. He wondered what it would be like to see the world from a point of view where there were no moral ambiguities, where every question was answered and each commandment had to be obeyed, whether logical or not.

Here was an explanation of why there were two kitchens in the rabbi's home. Ritual cleaning of year-round kitchens was required by Jewish law for Passover, so some more affluent Hasidim build second kitchens dedicated only for Passover to circumvent this exhausting yearly rite. He flipped a page. Hands had to be washed ritually before eating bread, thus an extra washbasin in the kitchen. Separation of meat and dairy products was required.

It occurred to him that any culture examined by outsiders must seem strange. The rituals of the Catholic Church, which he had been raised in, might seem bizarre to some. Orlando blinked thoughtfully, turned the page. Switching on any electrical apparatus was forbidden on the Sabbath—even automatic lights in refrigerators had to be clipped to keep them from coming on when the door was opened.

Here was something about sex. Married couples were not to touch at least two weeks out of the month. Then only after the wife immersed herself in a *mikvah*, a ritual bath, could intercourse take place.

He read on, fascinated. He wanted to see if there was any mention of the wig Menachem Rabowitz's wife wore when he had visited them. Yes, here. Married women frequently cut off most of their hair "for reasons of modesty" and wore wigs. Or they wore kerchiefs on their heads, for the same purpose.

Here was an explanation of why Hasidic men don't shave. It was against Jewish law, unholy . . . a sign of immorality.

Orlando thought for a moment, then froze. He slammed the book shut and stared blankly. He understood.

It was time to make an arrest.

The interrogation room wasn't much bigger than a closet. Chipped enamel paint, once a hard white but now fading to yellow, coated walls without windows. A lamp hung from the ceiling by a frayed black cord. The air was stale and hot, even this early in the morning. When the narrow door to the room opened, bringing with it a gust of fresh air, the lamp swayed, throwing dancing shadows around the room. Briggs stood in the doorway. He glanced at Menachem Rabowitz, gave Orlando a grunt, and shut the door behind him.

"So you got your man," Briggs said. His voice carried a ring of skepticism.

Orlando pushed a wooden chair in Briggs's direction. "Glad you could make it. We've just begun. He's waived his right to a lawyer for now. Says he just wants to clear things up and get this over as quickly as possible." Orlando couldn't help but smile. He'd made his point. He had brought Menachem Rabowitz in. He was conducting the interrogation. For the moment, this was his game; Briggs was here as an observer. Briggs had been wasting his time hunting for a kid who hid burglary tools in his closet.

"This is ludicrous." Menachem Rabowitz pounded his fist on the table in front of him. "I didn't kill my brother." The harsh light burning down on him cruelly accentuated his wrinkles and made black gashes of his eyes. His eyeglasses, glinting, lay on the table next to a recorder with tape spinning.

"Maybe you didn't plan to," Orlando said. "Maybe something just went wrong. Now tell me where you were the evening of the murder, and don't say you were with your wife."

"She'll testify to it."

Orlando pictured her in his mind: a face etched with worry. "And she'll be jailed for

perjury if she does. Would you like that?" He
turned to Briggs. "The Hasidim see shaving as
a mark of unholiness. The rabbi had screwed
his former sect again and again. They decided
to show the Hasidic world how evil he was by
forcibly shaving him. It was a form of public
humiliation."

Menachem Rabowitz leaned toward them.
"I had nothing to do with this murder."

"You had cause," Orlando persisted. "You
hated him. He took religious articles you consider sacred. We have witnesses who say you
people went crazy when he took that stuff.
Mrs. Rabowitz feared for the lives of her
children."

Menachem Rabowitz tried to move his chair
from the stark circle of light only to find it
was fastened to the floor. "What you say is
true, but I didn't kill him. If you're going to
arrest everyone who hated him, you'd better
start building more jails. You want motives for
me to kill him? I'll give you a hundred. I still
didn't do it."

"Then why all the lies?" Orlando said.
"Why not tell us where you were and what
you did on the night of the murder? Let me
tell you right now that if I was on a jury, I'd
vote to convict. You've lied from the first time
I saw you, and the evidence is piling up, and
it ain't in your favor."

"I didn't kill him," Menachem Rabowitz insisted. Sweat was beading on his forehead.
Dark splotches had formed at the armpits of

his white shirt. He reached over and turned off the recorder. In a whisper: "I'll tell you everything I *did* do if you guarantee me immunity from prosecution." He folded his arms and waited for Orlando's response.

"Don't make me laugh." Orlando rose and switched the recorder on. He leaned against the wall, arms akimbo.

"I know who bombed that abortion clinic! Drop any charges against me, and I'll give you the names of the men who did it."

Orlando and Briggs exchanged glances. This was a surprise. Orlando shook his head and scowled. "No deals. In the end, we'll get whatever information we want out of you anyway."

Menachem Rabowitz sat mute, staring at the floor. The only sound was the gentle whir of the tape recorder.

"First, you sent the shaving kit as a warning," Orlando prodded. "Perhaps his wife didn't understand, but Avraham Rabowitz did. He knew what it meant. And when that didn't stop him from selling more of the goods, you went after the shop owner. When he refused to capitulate to your demands, you vandalized his shop. And then you ritualistically shaved your brother to expose him as an unholy man, and then—"

"Yes, yes!" Menachem Rabowitz snapped, jumping up from his chair. "Everything you say is true. But we didn't kill him."

"Sit down," Orlando thundered. "You shaved him, and you slit his throat from ear to ear!"

"Never," Menachem Rabowitz hissed. "And I have witnesses."

"You shaved him, you slashed his throat, and you stuffed that prayer shawl down his throat."

Menachem Rabowitz dropped back in his chair. "You think I would use a religious garment to kill someone? That in itself proves no Jewish person committed this crime."

"You're not religious enough to refrain from murder, but you're too religious to use a prayer shawl?"

"I didn't kill him," Menachem Rabowitz said quietly. His shoulders sagged. "I did do the rest, but I didn't kill anybody."

"The whole story," Orlando demanded. "Now."

Menachem Rabowitz sighed. He rubbed his eyes and toyed with the eyeglasses on the table. "After we lost the court case, we felt there was nothing more we could do." He spoke dully, staring blankly at the tape recorder. He had the look of a man beaten down too many times. "We resolved to forget the matter, hurt as we were, but Avraham kept hitting on us. He went after our kids. Recruiting. A boy converted to his sect, then a couple more. The families were ripped apart. It was just the last straw. He had hurt us too much. You cannot imagine the rage we felt toward him. And now he was taking our children.

"He was an unholy man, and we decided to expose him for what he was. So we sent him that shaving kit as a warning. We thought he would come to his senses, if only out of fear. But Avraham persisted. We threatened his family. It accomplished nothing. We heard he was planning to sell off the last of our things. We warned the antique dealer, but he refused to heed our threats.

"On Monday night four of us nabbed Avraham on the street after he left that meeting with other members of his sect. We pulled him into the backseat of our car and stuffed a sock in his mouth. While one of us drove, the others held him down while I shaved his face. Avraham didn't struggle too hard after he got a couple of cuts on his fingers, not once I had the razor at his throat."

"What time was this?" Briggs was finally getting a word in. Orlando gave him a wry look. So he was interested now.

Menachem Rabowitz shrugged. "Around eleven-thirty. As we shaved Avraham, we told him why we were doing it—as if he didn't already know. We told him to leave our kids alone and to get the sacred articles back. We dropped him off several blocks from his house. Then the four of us drove over to the Brooklyn Bridge and threw the razor into the East River. We proceeded to the antique store on Seventy-second and Madison, and smashed the front window." He raised his hands. "And that's it. When you came to my door the next morning, I thought Avraham had called the police on us. I was stunned that he had been murdered."

"That's your story?" Orlando wasn't impressed.

"It's the truth. And I have witnesses. The other men will testify for me. We all went together. The papers say Avraham was killed about midnight. By that time we were on the Upper East Side breaking that window. Why would we have gone to the length of breaking in his back door and cutting him with the razor we sent to him when we could have done it in the car and dumped the body? We wanted to scare him, not kill him."

Orlando paced the room, his hand kneading his chin, thinking. He didn't like it, but he was beginning to believe Menachem Rabowitz. His story didn't solve the murder, but it made sense of the rest of the case. He glanced at his watch. Momentarily, he would know if Menachem Rabowitz and his cohorts were on the Upper East Side at the time of the murder.

Menachem Rabowitz put on his glasses. Clearing his throat, he said, "You think the district attorney will make a deal with me? I name the people who bombed that clinic and testify against them, in exchange for probation?"

Orlando shrugged. "If you're cleared of the murder charge, maybe. I can't say your testimony would be worth much under the circumstances, would you?"

"I have three other witnesses who saw them, too."

Orlando stopped pacing and leaned over the table. His hands gripped the edges. He frowned. "Okay, Rabowitz, out with it. What's this all about?"

Menachem Rabowitz spoke in a conspiratorial whisper. "Monday night was not the first time we tried to nab Avraham. We followed him to his meeting with his cronies the night before. They left in a group, so we didn't make our move. We wondered where they were going, so we followed. They went to that abortion clinic in Williamsburg, the one Avraham had been picketing. Avraham held something in a box. They must have had burglary tools because they got in the door in a snap. There was a lot of banging and crashing. They were there maybe twenty minutes, then slipped out. We had an inkling of what they might be doing, but it wasn't until the next day when I read about it in the paper that I knew for sure."

Orlando shook his head. "And you didn't bother to notify the police."

Menachem Rabowitz looked shame-faced. "It made us realize that we could shave Avraham without fear he would call the cops. It was our bargaining chip. When we were shaving him, we even brought up his little escapade to blackmail him into getting our things back."

"You can identify the men who were with him?"

Menachem Rabowitz nodded. "Yes, they

were all men from his synagogue. I don't know the names, but I know their faces."

Orlando reached for the door knob. "Okay, Rabowitz. I'll talk with the D.A.'s office. Maybe they'll cut a deal. You'll have to name your friends who were in on the shaving, and the D.A. will probably insist on cooperation from all of them, too. Frankly, I don't think Michel Serrout will want to press charges anyway, but I think you and your pals would look better if you offered to pay for the glass you broke."

Menachem Rabowitz nodded bleakly. "I'll do whatever you say. I just want to get back to my family."

Orlando pulled open the door, felt the rush of cool air in the hall with relief, and tilted his head back at Briggs. "You coming?"

CHAPTER 12

Briggs kicked the chair back and followed. Orlando gave instructions to the guard stationed in the hall, then turned to Briggs.

"I hate to say it, but I think he's telling the truth. It makes sense. It explains why we didn't find the hair from the rabbi's beard at the murder scene and why a different razor was used. Menachem Rabowitz and his gang dump the rabbi several blocks from his house after shaving him, and he staggers home. Once inside, he puts his hand to his face and gets blood on it. He goes through the dining room, smudging the switch with blood as he turns the light on, then goes to the bathroom to wash up. That's why we found traces of blood and some hairs in the sink."

Orlando looked up. Mrs. Burdict bustled toward them, her hair a bright flame in the otherwise monochrome hallway. She hugged a folder stuffed with Xeroxed clippings.

"You're a hard man to find," she said with the gentle scolding tone of a mother talking to a child who has eaten too much cotton candy at a fair. "And I worked so hard to get these for you yesterday." She blinked her magnified eyes through thick lenses.

Orlando knew it was best to accommodate Mrs. Burdict, to stroke her motherly instincts. "I'm sorry, Mrs. Burdict. I should have called in at the end of the day to see if you had anything for me, shouldn't I?"

She appeared mollified and handed him the folder. "That's it, the whole caboodle."

"You're a lifesaver, Mrs. Burdict. I'd like you to do me a favor. When Barlow and Stone come looking for me, send them to the lounge."

Mrs. Burdict glanced at Briggs, pursed her lips in distaste, then nodded at Orlando. She had the look of a mother who disapproves of her child's friends.

All eyes focused on them when they entered the lounge, looked away, then did a double take. There would be talk in the locker room tonight, Orlando thought. He poured two cups of coffee, handed one to Briggs, and they found a table scattered with crumbs in the corner. Orlando drew back a chair and settled in. He was enjoying the stunned look on the faces across the room.

"No sugar," Briggs muttered, set his cup down, and snatched a packet from a bowl on the next table. He sat, ripped open the packet, and dumped its contents into the cup. He looked at Orlando appraisingly. "When I heard you brought Menachem Rabowitz in for questioning, I knew you were way off the mark. Men like that don't commit this sort of crime."

Orlando shrugged. "Well, at least we'll get the men who bombed that clinic behind bars. The ones who are still living, that is. And we learned a lot about the Rabowitz case. It almost looks like a simple burglary gone sour, except—"

"That's why I say the punk did it—Rodriguez. It was like you said. Rabowitz stumbles home after the shaving, and cleans up in his bathroom. He hears something in the bedroom. He goes to investigate. Little Jimmy Rodriguez is there, ransacking the room for jewelry, whatever. Rodriguez panics—Rabowitz can identify him—he grabs the razor from the bureau and slashes the rabbi in the ensuing scuffle."

"Except for the prayer shawl. Jimmy Rodriguez didn't stuff that down his throat. No, there's a piece missing here. By the way, did they find any of Jimmy Rodriguez's fingerprints in Rabowitz's bedroom?"

Briggs shook his head and tasted the coffee. He pushed back his chair and went to the next table. This time he brought the bowl of sugar packets back and plunked it on the table. He took his seat and poured another packet in his coffee. "No. But we figured he was wearing gloves, since there were no prints on the razor. But think about it. Why else would he run? When we catch the little bastard, you'll see.

And remember the burglary tools. I say that's proof enough."

"Yeah," Orlando drawled. "Too bad we can't use them in court."

Barlow and Stone stepped into the room, saw Orlando with Briggs, looked hesitant. Orlando waved them over. "You got something for me?"

Barlow was the taller of the two, with short cropped black hair and smooth olive skin. He said, "Several people heard the crash at midnight. There are a lot of apartments above the shops on that street. The time seems pretty accurate. A couple said they looked at their clocks when it happened. They were pissed to be woke up at that hour. We only found one person who said she saw the incident. She said they were Hasidic Jews—four of them."

Stone stepped forward. He had sandy hair and a nose that started out narrow then became bulbous. "She's willing to try to pick them out of a police lineup, but said she isn't sure how much help she'll be. She said they all look so much alike."

Orlando thanked the officers, and they left. He emptied his cup and pushed back his chair.

"What do you think?" Briggs asked.

Orlando made a sound in his throat. "I think that pretty well cinches it. It's clear where they were at the time of the murder."

Briggs stared at his coffee cup. "It's possible Menachem Rabowitz stayed behind while the others trashed that shop."

Orlando shook his head. "I don't think so. It just doesn't hold together. I don't believe Rabowitz would have used that prayer shawl to gag his brother to death." He rose and picked up the folder Mrs. Burdict had given him.

"Where are you off to?"

Orlando waved the folder and grimaced. "I've got some reading to do. When I'm done, I'll drop by your office." But he wouldn't. He'd spent the last couple days dodging Briggs, and today wouldn't be any different.

Orlando was halfway up the main stairway of the station house when he heard a vaguely familiar raspy female voice raised in anger. He turned and saw the red beret. The sergeant behind the main desk was pointing his finger. His cheeks were flushed.

"You heard me, lady. I said you can't bring that dog in here."

Donese Jones stood with her hands on her hips. Her bony little boys hid behind her, hanging on the pleats of her coat. Runyon, canine muscles bulging, produced a snarl and sharp fangs to go with it.

"Why? He's not hurting you, is he?"

Saliva dripped in silvery threads from Runyon's mouth.

"Is that a Seeing Eye dog, lady? If it isn't, then it's against the rules to bring him in here." He hiked a thumb in the air. "Get that dog outside."

"And where am I supposed to put him? I'm

not tying Runyon outside and having someone come along and steal him from me. This dog cost money."

Runyon bared his teeth and let out a growl. "No one is going to touch your dog, trust me." The telephone on the desk jangled, and the sergeant spoke into the receiver.

"This is just so typical," Donese fumed. Her voice rose, though she was speaking to no one in particular. "You can't even walk down the street in this city without getting socked in the face, and you cops are more concerned with where my dog goes than catching the creep who attacked me! Damn!"

Orlando called down to her and she turned, her face hard with scorn. Recognition flooded her face and her features softened, then sharpened with wariness. She did not look necessarily glad to see him.

Orlando descended the stairs, but kept his distance in deference to Runyon, whose throat rumbled with the warning of a growl. "You remember me, Detective Orlando," he said.

"Oh, I remember you." The light brown eyes with hazel chips looked sullen. "You catch that rabbi killer yet?"

"Not yet."

"You people aren't much good at catching anybody, are you? Can't even come here to report a crime without being hassled for having a dog."

"Why don't you tie him outside? There's a

railing along the steps. Then we can take care of this."

A disgruntled frown creased her face, but she grabbed the dog by the collar and pulled him out the door. The little boys stood in drab oversized coats staring at the checkered pattern of the linoleum floor, their shoulders slumped. They looked like a couple of scarecrows draped in gunny sacks. Orlando put his hand on the older boy's shoulder, but he jerked away.

"Shouldn't you kids be in school?"

Duane, the older boy, scuffed his tennis shoe on the floor in answer. Brian said, "Mom needs us to protect her. Somebody socked her, right in the nose!"

"It wasn't the nose," Duane scowled, jabbing his brother with an elbow. "It was like right under the eye." He struck his fist in an open hand. "Man, if I catch that guy that hit Mom, I'm gonna strangle him to death."

"I'm going to shoot him to death!" Brian cried.

"You kids shut up." Donese stood above them. She gave Orlando a cold stare. "If that dog gets stole, you're gonna pay for a new one."

Orlando grinned wryly. "I think Runyon is safe from any dog nappers lurking outside the station house." Then he noticed the purple splotch spread across her cheek. "Tell me what happened."

"I was just walking to the grocery store,

minding my own business, when this guy walks straight up to me and belts me in the face. Like, he socks me with all his might."

"You didn't have Runyon with you?"

She chuckled sourly. "They don't let dogs in the grocery store either."

"The kids?"

"They was with my mother."

"What did the man look like?"

"It was a white guy."

Orlando blinked. "Did he have a face? Features?"

"He looked like some guy in a magazine ad. Blond. He had a business suit on. The guy looked like a stockbroker, but big. Arnold Schwarzenegger big."

"He walked up and hit you, and then what?"

"The motherfucker knocked me to the ground, he hit me so hard, and then he jumped in a car and they sped off."

"What kind of car?"

"A big black thing. There had to be at least two of them, because the bastard that hit me jumped in the backseat, so someone else was driving."

"License plate?"

"Shit no. I was sprawled on the sidewalk seeing stars."

"Anyone else around who might have seen what happened?"

She shook her head. "I didn't see no one—" Her arms fastened to her hips. "Don't tell me you're going to claim it didn't happen. White guy attacks a black woman, and nobody's interested. I got proof it happened, and it's on my face." Her index finger became a dagger that pointed to the bruise.

"I'm not questioning that. I just need information. Did this all just happen?"

"Yesterday." She crossed her arms defiantly.

"Yesterday?" Orlando shook his head. "Why didn't you come sooner?"

"I almost didn't come at all, and seeing how things are going, I shouldn't of bothered."

"Any ideas why someone would have it in for you?"

"You tell me. Things was going fine till you popped into my life."

Orlando led the way down a hall and to an officer who could handle the complaint.

"I don't even know why I'm doing this. Nothing going to be done anyway." The boys huddled at her side.

"Don't be too sure," Orlando said. He left her and the kids, and returned to his office, the folder tight under his arm.

He had some reading to do.

The syringe was small and narrow, with an orange plunger. It lay between two squat bottles labeled R and N, and glistened in the pool of light from the halogen lamp on the desk. Designer blinds were shut tight against the storm clouds brewing on the horizon. Herb Chiligny took the syringe in one hand, one of the bottles in the other, turned it upside down, squinted, pierced the membrane with the needle, and drew a quantity of medicine.

"I hope you don't mind," he said. "Some people aren't used to seeing this kind of thing. I've been doing it all my life, and I'll never get used to the bother. But it's either this or unpleasant alternatives." He pulled liquid from the second bottle, then said, "You don't have to look if you don't want to." He exposed a flabby tanned stomach with a curl of black hair above the belly button, then grabbed a roll of fat and buried the needle in it. "That's that." Orlando heard the syringe clank into a Sharps container under the desk.

Chiligny rose, found his cane, clasped the bottles in his free hand, and limped across his office to the closet. A portable refrigerator lay inside, under a rack of expensive coats and suit jackets. He bent, put the medicine in the refrigerator, plucked a brown bag from inside, and returned to the desk. "The hardest part of the whole thing was when I was a teenager. They used to pick on me in school, saying I was a drug addict. Or, 'dope addict,' as they said in the small town where I was raised." He settled in his padded chair, put the bag on the green blotter, and slipped the cane under the desk. "I don't suppose kids are any kinder today, what with needles and the fear of AIDS."

Orlando leaned in the doorway. "Chiligny, we've got to talk." He held the folder stuffed with newspaper articles under his arm.

"Don't tell me you've been reading my column." Chiligny put his palm to his mouth in mock concern. "It's so bad for one's morals."

Orlando dropped into a chair and slapped the folder down on the desk. "It's not my morals I'm worried about. Why didn't you come clean when I saw you Tuesday? You and Rabowitz were in a fist fight on the floor of the city council chambers."

Chiligny leaned back in his chair. A grin spread across his round face. "So that's why you're here. And I thought you'd come for a social call." Eyelashes batted. "I did a little checking up on you. I was happy to hear that you're—what's the quaint way of putting it?— 'on the bus.' "

"Do I have to tell you to cut the bullshit every time I see you?"

Chiligny attempted a contrite expression. "No, sorry. But I do so love to hear a lion roar. When you get gruff, it just sends shivers right down my spine."

Orlando grunted. "The council hearings. Tell me about it."

The doe eyes went serious. "I can't even recall the year it happened. We went down to the council so many times over a period of fifteen years to get that bill passed."

"I have the article here," Orlando said. He leaned forward and leafed through the folder.

Chiligny waved his hand. "Doesn't matter. The same thing happened every year. We'd get up and speak in favor of the bill, and the bigots would testify against it. If I remember right, Rabowitz was referring to it as the Pervert Lifestyle Bill that year. When he got his turn at the podium, he claimed that when a gay man can't find another gay man to have sex with—Heaven forbid—we do it with animals! Great imagination that man had. When he went back to his seat, I walked over and told him that the only one who was into bestiality was his wife."

Orlando could hardly suppress a smile.

A sheepish grin broke out on Chiligny's face. "I must admit, I do produce some great zingers now and then. Anyway, our conversation deteriorated, and pretty soon we were scuffling on the floor. If I recall correctly, I bit a good chunk out of his ear."

"And that was it? No arrests?"

Chiligny shook his head. "Our respective groups pulled us apart, and sat us at opposite corners of the room like children in a schoolyard fray. Tempers would run high at those hearings. Our fracas was par for the course."

"You ever see him again?"

"At least once a year. He'd always be across from St. Patrick's on Gay Day protesting our existence. But I never got the opportunity to throttle him again, if that's what you mean." He tossed up his hands. "Look, if you threw the book at me for every person whose eyes I've scratched out over the last twenty-five years, I'd be in Sing-Sing till Hell freezes over."

"What about Leonard Lynch?"

"You *have* been reading my column, Detective Orlando. No, I haven't been able to get close enough to Lynch to take his eyes out. But I'm letting my nails grow just in case."

"Your paper has devoted a lot of copy to him."

"He deserves it. He's one of the most glamorous—and dangerous—men in the city. He has about as much compassion for other people as your garden-variety psychopath. That's a man who thinks nothing of making old people homeless to make a few bucks. We had a major campaign here at the paper to stop him from taking over Times Square. In a city with tens of thousands of homeless people, Lynch wanted to tear down existing apartment buildings to erect luxury high rises for his friends."

He indicated the bag on the desk. "You don't mind if I eat? Actually, I'm supposed to wait awhile after taking my insulin shot, but I find ignoring medical advice as much as possible so satisfying, don't you?"

"When did all this stuff with Lynch happen?"

Chiligny opened the bag and produced a salad in a plastic deli container. "Last year. Well, it was like this: Lynch found land prices for his proposed commercial center too high down on Wall Street, so he searched high and low in the island of Manhattan for another neighborhood to pillage. He figured he could buy up dilapidated old Times Square and do a make-over on it. He thought he'd get good press for rehabilitating the area." Chiligny groped in the bag for a plastic fork. "He thought wrong."

"What was the problem?"

Chiligny speared a miniature tomato, plopped it in his mouth, squashed it under wide teeth. "He didn't have any room in his big plans for all the people he was going to displace. He thought no one would notice all the poor and old people who'd be kicked out into the street if he got his way." His eyes went hard. "I noticed."

"And so you wrote about it in your column."

"That's how it started. Then I did a piece for the front page of the *Village World*. It became a series of articles. Then other papers picked up on it. The Coalition for the Homeless staged protests in front of Lynch Towers. When the *New York Times* ran an editorial criticizing Lynch's plan, we knew we had won. The city leaders wouldn't touch it with a ten-foot pole." Chiligny munched with satisfaction.

"And what became of Lynch's plan for a commercial center?"

Chiligny shrugged. "You tell me."

Orlando rose and picked up the folder on the desk. "In a couple of hours, I may be able to do just that."

CHAPTER 13

A cold rain whispered against the floor-to-ceiling windows of the Lynch Enterprises reception area. Dull clouds, ominous and heavy, burdened the skyline. Wind brushed the sides of the tower with a low steady whistle. It was only one-fifteen, but an early dusk had settled over the city. Wall-to-wall windows were not enough to brighten the room and lighted panels shone down to artificially illuminate what nature could not. The elevator door closed behind Orlando, and his shoes dug into a thick carpet with Oriental motifs. He knew that his arrival had been announced. The moment he approached the penthouse elevator on the ground floor, showing his badge, a phone call had been made to the top of the tower.

Every eye in the room was on him. The secretary leaned forward from behind the desk, pointed padded shoulders accentuating the angularity of her body. She blinked eyelashes thick with mascara. The bodyguards watched him with studied confidence. Orlando remembered what Donese Jones had said. Yes, they

looked like stockbrokers in their expensive
suits. Models in a magazine advertisement.
Again, the cameras in the corners of the room
stared at him. Orlando strode to the desk.

"I'm here to see Leonard Lynch."

Her eyes squinted as she scanned the book
in front of her. "Hmmm. I seem to remember
you didn't make an appointment on your last
visit."

"Cut the bullshit." He whipped a folded
piece of paper from his coat, opened it, flattened it on the desk with thick fingers. "A
warrant to question your boss. I don't need
your permission." Orlando's thumb covered
the spot where Mrs. Burdict had signed her
name as the presiding judge.

"Too bad you went to all that trouble," she
said casually, a thin smile spreading across
her face—a curve incongruous among all the
straight lines. "Mr. Lynch is out of town. Will
be until next week. Could you come back
then?"

It was Orlando's turn to smile. He pulled a
second order from his pocket and spread it
on the desk. "Search warrant. I don't care
whether Lynch is here or not." He pointed to
the inner office door behind her. "I'm going in
that door." As he stuffed the warrants back in
his pocket, Orlando felt the guards surround
him. *Feeding frenzy time.* He turned to face
them.

"The lady says he isn't here. What could
you possibly want rummaging through Mr.

Lynch's things?" He was big, blond. His hands curled into meaty fists at his sides.

"That's not really your business, is it?" Orlando snorted, reached out, and flipped Big Blond's tie. "Your duds don't fool me. I know what you are. Stick to beating up on poor women. That's more your style."

A fist the size of a ham gripped Orlando's wrist. "Don't push me, buddy. I make Mr. Lynch's business my business."

"Spoken like a true lackey. Now remove your hand, or I'll have you on the floor with your wrists cuffed behind your back and a Smith & Wesson at your temple."

Big Blond grinned and exchanged glances with the other guards. They grinned back. "You wanna try me?"

"Sure. Let's see if you can handle more than a woman half your size."

The door to the inner office flew open. Orlando twisted his head back. Leonard Lynch stood in the doorway. Orlando recognized him from television, but had never realized how short the entrepreneur was. Television exposure did that to people, made them big. Despite his height, Lynch carried the imposing stature of a man who was powerful and knew it. He was dressed in an impeccable gray suit with a red tie. His voice boomed.

"MacNamara, go cool off."

The fist gripping Orlando's wrist withered and so did the grin. MacNamara disappeared through a door by the elevator like a sulking

third grader sent from the classroom for bad
behavior.

Lynch stepped forward. His demeanor
changed, like one mask substituted for another.
He was all smiles and charm from his capped
white teeth to his twinkling gray eyes. "So you
must be the notorious Detective Orlando." He
raised his hand and summoned Orlando to
him, curling his arm around the detective as
if they were old friends. Orlando recalled that
the social page said Lynch dripped with
charm when it was in his interest.

Orlando was shown into the office, and
Lynch closed the door behind them. He gave
Orlando a pat on the back and said, "Let me
take that." Orlando shed his coat, and Lynch
slipped open a closet door and hung it inside.

The office was expansive, its spaciousness
accentuated by walls of windows that made
the room seem to reach the far horizon. Despite the brooding clouds outside threatening
violence, the office was bright and cheerful.
Starkly but beautifully furnished, it boasted a
Brancusi sculpture on a pedestal and a small
Rodin bronze on the coffee table. Two massive
Oriental vases flanked an overstuffed couch.
Lynch's mammoth desk was littered with papers and three phones. Orlando had been
right: a series of small television screens were
set into the desk, picturing the reception area,
the lobby, and other parts of the building Orlando didn't recognize. Lynch knew everything that went on in this building. Medieval

tapestries matched the ones in the reception area. Orlando examined the weave, the deep red and blue colors faded but still majestic.

Lynch shut the closet door. He smiled faintly. "I wanted to buy the *Dame à la Licorne* tapestry. The one with the unicorn and the lady. I was told by the French government that it was priceless, not for sale." Lynch winked. "So you see, there are things that even I can't buy."

Orlando looked at him pointedly. "Yeah, a few things. Still, it takes some guts to ask a government to sell one of its national treasures."

Lynch chuckled. "Guts? Hell, say what you mean. It takes unmitigated gall, it takes arrogance to pull a stunt like that. And I have arrogance in spades, Detective Orlando. If I didn't, I wouldn't be where I am today." He stepped to a low-lying cabinet and pulled open finely carved Oriental doors. "Please take a seat. What would you like to drink?"

"Nothing. I'm on duty." Orlando sank into the couch.

"Oh, come on, Detective Orlando, I won't tell." Lynch set two glasses on the cabinet. Ice rattled in the glasses, then he splashed Scotch on top. Orlando didn't have to be told that it was the best brand. Lynch swept up the glasses and joined him on the couch. He handed one to Orlando, who took the glass and set it on the coffee table.

"Ah," Lynch said. "A man who cannot be compromised or corrupted. I like that."

"Like your friend MacNamara?"

Lynch blew out a snort of contempt. "Sorry about him. He's not 'too smart, but he's loyal as an old dog, as my father used to say. And in my position, you need men like that." He took a sip of Scotch, closed his eyes for a moment and savored its taste. "Man, that's good. You really should try it. You know, I think that's the best thing about having money. It's not the expensive cars or the mansions, it's the good food and drink that I enjoy the most." He settled back in the cushions. "Now what did you want to speak to me about?"

"How about the price of real estate in Manhattan?"

Lynch blinked. He set the glass on the coffee table. He brushed boyish bangs aside casually, but his face went tense. "Surely you didn't come here to discuss what you could learn from the real estate section of the *New York Times*."

"Some stories never make it to the newspapers. You of all people should know that."

Lynch raised his glass from the table and took a long sip. "I'm a straightforward man. Let's don't dance around. Ask me what you want to know."

"Tell me about Forty-second Street."

Lynch let out a laugh. "Oh, Forty-second Street. No secret there. *That* was on the front page of the *New York Times*."

"And in the *Village World*."

Lynch snickered. He rubbed his thumb along the beveled edges of the glass in his hand, studying the distorted light it created, as if it carried more interest than the conversation. "So you've been reading that rag." He mimicked a namby-pamby voice. " 'Evil Leonard Lynch throws sick old people out on the street so he can tear down their homes of thirty years to build high-priced office space.' " He growled. "Yeah, I know the philosophy of that paper. It's a great publication for people who need to live off other people's achievements. What Ayn Rand called 'the looters.' " He downed his drink.

"The city *did* give you forty million in tax breaks."

His eyes, hard as steel, met Orlando's. "That's beside the point. What I do is good for this city. If New York doesn't keep growing, it will die. The people who run this city don't seem to understand that simple fact.

"Take my efforts to revitalize Forty-second Street, for example. I had a plan to turn that pimp-infested porn hole called Times Square into a vibrant business and entertainment center where people could go at night without being tormented to buy drugs or sex. But no, that would ruin the flavor, *the flavor*, of the neighborhood. So said your do-gooder *Village World* types.

"That Herb Chiligny was the worst. Ever get a look at that guy?" Lynch flipped a limp wrist and snickered. "So he and his coalition-for-the-homeless types get on a bandwagon to fight against my plan. They wanted the old buildings restored and used to warehouse street people. That'll sure bring new business to this city!" He shook his head in disgust. "And I used to give money to their cause." He went to the cabinet. Ice clinked in his glass, and he poured from the bottle of Scotch. When he turned, Orlando saw color had come to his face.

Lynch smiled sheepishly. "Sorry, but this whole thing just makes my blood boil. And with the prices for land in Wall Street, forget it. The city wants to attract new business, but isn't willing to buck the special interest groups and let me build the office space."

"You could always go to Brooklyn," Orlando said. "Williamsburg for instance. Just over the bridge. Comparatively inexpensive. Renters have no power in this city. You could easily throw them out. And landowners would profit from having Williamsburg a business center."

Small lines appeared between Lynch's brows. "I don't know what you mean."

"But first," Orlando continued, "you'd have to find a go-between. If word got out that Leonard Lynch was buying land in Williamsburg to turn it into a commercial center to rival Wall Street, think how prices would rise. No, I'm afraid you'd have to have someone, someone trusted by the community, someone already known as a landowner in Williamsburg, to do your dirty work for you. To get the zoning changed and to option all that land. Someone willing to work for a measly fee—because let's face it, rich people are the cheapest of all—but with the knowledge that his own holdings in Williamsburg would increase mightily in value once your plans became a reality."

The color had drained from Lynch's cheeks. His eyes narrowed. "What do you want?"

"How about the truth? What deal did you have with the rabbi?"

Lynch took a gulp from his glass, then strolled to the windows. He stared out at the dimness. "You know," he said quietly, "this is all conjecture. You don't have a shred of paper linking me with Rabowitz."

"I have a search warrant. I can rifle through your files if you'd like."

He turned and looked sharply at Orlando. "You won't find anything."

"Maybe not, but I can sure make your office a mess."

"If you persist in this, I'm going to call the mayor again and have you served at the next mayor's dinner with an apple in your mouth and a spit up your ass."

"That wouldn't be smart. The newspapers would want to know why the mayor was obstructing a murder investigation."

"I don't think you understand who you're dealing with." The eyes were savage. "I eat guys like you for breakfast. I didn't make it where I am today without stepping on people. Do you realize how much power I have?"

"I have power, too."

Lynch scoffed. "Your badge?"

"That. And the newspapers. Think of how much they'd love to hear about your plans for Williamsburg. Talk about front-page news."

"I own the papers in this town."

"You don't own the *Village World,* and you don't own Herb Chiligny."

"I could buy that rag in a second and line my trash can with it."

"If you were innocent, why would you have to?"

Lynch drew a deep breath, let the air out in a sigh. He seemed to weigh his options. Finally, he said, "Okay, I'm going to cooperate with you because I've done nothing wrong. I just want you out of my life. Now, what do you want to know?"

"The deal. Tell me about the deal."

Lynch shrugged and looked at his glass. "It was like you said. I realized Williamsburg could be the location of my business center. I knew land prices would soar if there was even a whisper that I was interested, so I engaged the rabbi as my agent. No one would blink an eye when he optioned land there and filed to change the zoning."

"You're telling me what I already know, Lynch. Why not just set up a dummy corporation?"

Lynch shook his head and smiled ruefully. "No, that would have fueled rumors. Rabowitz was known in that community. It was the perfect deal."

"But something went wrong."

"Nothing went wrong with the deal. Because Rabowitz was murdered, I'm without an agent. That's all. A temporary setback." Lynch's jaw went rigid, and his eyes burned. "And you can just keep your fucking mouth shut, buster, because I'm not losing out on a multimillion-dollar deal because some cop wants to make captain. You expose that deal to the papers, and I'll show you what a mean motherfucker I can be." He jabbed a finger in the air.

"Is that what you told Rabowitz when he double-crossed you? Is that why you murdered him?"

Lynch looked incredulous. "Are you crazy? This has nothing to do with him. Just shut the fuck up about the Williamsburg deal, you hear?"

"You think I care about your back-room deals? You should be more concerned whether I'm going to haul your ass down to the station house and mess up your fingers with ink, 'cause you're a prime suspect, and our conversation just reinforces all my suspicions about you. You better get straight with me, Lynch, and quick. We're talking a murder rap here."

Lynch threw his glass across the room. It crashed against the wall, leaving a splatter of Scotch. "Fuck! What's that stupid Jew got to do with me? I didn't kill him. He just optioned some land for me for a fee."

"That's not the whole story. What happened?"

Lynch stared blankly at the carpet, breathing heavily. "The little bastard wanted ten percent of everything. Ten percent of the land, ten percent of the office buildings I would erect. I told him he was nothing more than a piddling agent, a go-between as you would say, and the fee we had agreed upon before was more than sufficient. He refused to budge, and I washed my hands of him. I told him I'd just find another agent. That's it."

"And lose out on all that seed money you'd given him to option the land? C'mon, Lynch. There's more. I can see it in your beady eyes."

Lynch paced, his shoulders sagging. "He said he'd expose the whole deal and ruin it for me. He'd go to the media, and everyone would know I planned to create a new business district in Williamsburg. The prices would skyrocket, and that would be the end of my plan to buy cheap land there. But I didn't kill him. Can you imagine me with a straight razor?"

"No," Orlando said quietly. "But I can imagine you sending one of your thugs to do it. How did you put it? A person in your position needs men like that."

"I'm a businessman," Lynch said. He stopped pacing, stooped, and picked up the shards of his glass scattered on the carpet. He brought them to a wastebasket by the desk and gently set them at the bottom. He looked up at Orlando. "Not a murderer. And I defy you to prove different."

Orlando put his palms on his knees and

pushed up from the couch. "One thing I do know. MacNamara or one of your other flunkies assaulted a woman you wanted to shut up. I say you ordered him to do it." He got his coat from the closet, opened the office door, and turned back. "And I'm going to nail you both for it."

"Don't count on it," Lynch said under his breath, carefully brushing off the hand that held the pieces of glass. "I haven't played my last card yet."

The crowd of fifty blacks was loud and angry, chanting in the otherwise deserted street in front of the Rabowitz home. No doubt the throng would have been bigger except for the rain, which came down in sweeping torrents. A few had umbrellas, but the rest seemed fueled by the downpour that soaked their clothes and turned their placards limp and soggy. The Reverend Melvin Packard led the group in a circle, shouting, "Two, four six, eight, the neighborhood patrol means *hate, hate, hate!*" A news crew had just parked across the street.

Just what we need, Orlando thought. *The media to fan the flames*. He curbed his car and got out. Rain pelted his face. When he had called Mrs. Burdict from uptown for any messages, he was given Briggs's blunt order: *Get over to the rabbi's place quick*. Now he could see why. This case didn't need any more complications, and Briggs was the last man anyone would choose to diffuse a volatile racial situation. Not with his reputation. Orlando recognized Briggs's Plymouth parked up the street, and walked over and rapped on the window.

"Where the fuck have you been?" Briggs hollered, rolling down the window a crack. "You know we're supposed to work together on this case."

"Still? And here I thought you'd already solved the case and done your own special brand of search and seizure." Orlando gripped the door handle. "Why are you cowering in there? Afraid of the rain?"

Briggs scowled. "Fuck you. You know what happens if I show my face in front of those people. They're the ones who were screaming for my head at the grand jury investigation. You talk to them."

Orlando pulled open the car door. "But you forget. We're a team. Buddies. Partners. C'mon, you wimp. Face the music." He grabbed Briggs's shoulders and yanked him from the car. "Now, are you going to walk, or do I drag you over there?"

Briggs's eyes glistened with hate. "You're gonna pay, Orlando. Someday, when your back is turned, you're gonna pay."

" 'When your back is turned,' " Orlando shook his head. "The key phrase of your existence. Why did you come here to begin with if you plan to hide in your car?"

"One of the neighbors called me—I gave them all my card when I questioned them about the murder—and said maybe Rabowitz's killer was in the crowd. I didn't realize Packard and his apes would be here."

Orlando looked at Briggs with disgust. "These people aren't killers. They're angry and they're frustrated, but they have nothing to do with the murder."

The two cops stood back until the news crew had interviewed Packard and sped away to edit the story for the five-o'clock telecast. Orlando eschewed talking with the press. He had learned long ago that they had their own agenda, and it didn't always mesh with keeping peace in the city. One thing he didn't need now was the TV news playing up a racial angle on the case that might not exist.

Reverend Packard crossed the street toward them, not seeming to notice the puddles he was splashing through. His eyes were riveted on Briggs. "I recognize you!" he said in a booming voice. He was heavyset with broad shoulders and short hair slicked back with oil. "You're the one that murdered that Willis boy!" He thrust a finger in the air.

"I don't need this," Briggs said. "You talk to this clown. Use my car to get out of the rain. I'll go down the street and wait in yours." He turned on his heel and stalked off.

"Who's the clown?" Packard yelled after him. "Who you calling a clown?"

"Forget it," Orlando said. He showed his badge. "Let's get out of the rain, huh?"

Packard looked at him suspiciously, but followed him to the Plymouth. Orlando slipped into the driver's seat and unlocked the passenger side. Packard got inside and slammed the door. Raindrops hung on his forehead. "I hope you don't think you can get away with anything, not when I have fifty of my people across the street."

"Look," Orlando said. "I just don't want any trouble. I'm investigating the Rabowitz murder, and I don't see any racial issues involved here."

"I don't care about that murder," Packard snapped. "It's none of my business. What *is* my business is a neighborhood vigilante squad made up exclusively of Jews that exists to harass blacks."

Orlando made a face. "That neighborhood patrol is a lot of talk. When they realize how much time and effort it takes, they won't bother."

"They already have one in Crown Heights. All white. A black boy can't even walk down the street without getting flashed by the searchlight from one of their patrol cars."

"Don't you think this demonstration is just going to increase tensions?"

"I think when a gang of Jewish boys—followers of that dead rabbi, by the way—burn down the house of a black woman, that raises tensions."

Orlando sighed and shook his head. "Those boys were arrested this morning. They did a terrible thing, but don't blame the whole community for what a few punks did."

"Oh, but I *do* blame the whole community." Packard's voice rose, taking on the mannered tone he used in the pulpit, and Orlando could see why he was famed for galvanizing the disenfranchised into a seething mass. "Are those Hymie punks going to be tried for the attempted murder of an entire black family? *No!* The D.A.'s office is charging them on some piddling attempted arson rap. You see, when a Hymie tries to kill some niggers, that's not attempted murder in the eyes of the law."

"You think when Jews hear that kind of language it helps the situation?"

"You think I care about their paranoia?" Packard spat out. "It doesn't disturb you, does it, that a black man can't even walk in many neighborhoods in this city without being harassed? Those Jews are so touchy, you can't even use the word 'Jew' without getting them offended. You got to say 'Jewish.' And you'd better say it with a smile."

"Stick to the subject. How about if you met with the leaders of the patrol, and they agreed to integrate? What would you have against blacks and Jews working together to keep the neighborhood safe?" The truth was, Orlando couldn't picture it, not with fear and hostility running so high. But he had to try. "I'm not kidding myself that it would overcome the racial tension in this community, but it would be a start."

Packard waved his hand in dismissal. "Never happen. This is a power thing. Jews over blacks. 'Integrate' is a word they don't understand in this neighborhood. It's like two foreign countries living in the same crowded spot. Different schools for the kids, different stores, you could even say we have a different language."

"I refuse to believe these people are all that bad. They're frightened. They've just had a murder on their street. Meet with them. Tell them your concerns. Can a little communication hurt this situation?"

Packard shrugged. "I'll meet with them." A smile crept onto his face. "If they'll meet with me." His face went hard again. "But the protests don't stop till they integrate or disband."

Orlando nodded. "I truly believe we can diffuse this problem before it erupts into more violence."

Packard threw him a look of skepticism, then pushed the door open and stepped into the rain.

An Oldsmobile sped down the street, a blur of fedoras in the rain-smeared windows. "Go home, you crack-head niggers!" a frantic voice from within screamed. Then the car zoomed off, leaving a fantail of spray in its wake.

Packard bent and looked Orlando in the eye. "You truly believe," he scoffed and slammed the door.

The rain had slowed to a drizzle as Orlando drove down State Street toward home. He was glad he and Stewart had talked the night before, cleared the air. Maybe nothing had been solved, but he felt better. Perhaps some of the stresses on a relationship were never smoothed out, just handled day to day. And that was okay. He knew that next time he needed comfort, he'd reach for Stewart, not a bottle of rum.

At the stoplight, he read his watch. Almost three. He still had to get back to the station house later, but the idea of a late lunch with Stewart—and who knows what else?—had taken hold as he left the scene of the protest.

Briggs had given him a self-satisfied smirk when Orlando slipped from behind the wheel of the Plymouth, then slunk into the car and drove off. It was all so unlike Briggs. He was a coward all right, but not that kind of coward. Oh, he would use his authority as a cop to taunt those he didn't like, and Briggs had already proved unarmed minorities weren't safe when he had a gun in his hand. But he wasn't one to back down and walk away, especially in an altercation with blacks. Briggs had uncharacteristically played the wimp, and Orlando wondered why. He may have been afraid of the wrath of fifty angry blacks, but turning and running was not his way. Whipping his gun out would have been a more likely reaction.

The light turned green, and Orlando stepped on the gas. He couldn't shake the strange feeling someone had put something over on him. That obnoxious smile Briggs had

tossed his way after Orlando had spoken with
Packard . . .

Then a thought occurred to him. He remembered how Briggs had tried to get him to leave
his coat in the Plymouth when the two men
had spoken with Michael Greenberg. To plant
something? Orlando swerved the Chevy to the
curb. He couldn't believe what he was thinking, but the fact that Briggs had offered him
the use of his Plymouth to confer with Packard weighed heavily on his mind. There had
to be a reason. Briggs would probably scrub
the spot the reverend sat on with alcohol. Why
the niceties for two men he hated?

Orlando punched the glove compartment
door. It popped open, and he rummaged through
registration papers, gum wrappers, and an as-
sortment of pencils and pens. No, Briggs
wouldn't have made it so easy. Orlando
reached down and patted under the seat. His
hand brushed over a bump in the carpet, and
he worked his fingers into a jagged slit nearby.
He pulled out a plastic sack bulging with
white powder. Orlando shook with anger.
Briggs had probably already made an anony-
mous tip to Narcotics. He pocketed the
cocaine.

Lunch with Stewart was out. Orlando shoved
the car in gear, glanced out the rearview mirror, gassed the car, and pulled a sharp U-turn.

Briggs had just arrived home a moment before Orlando banged on his door. Standing in

the open doorway, his coat still stained with wet patches on the shoulders, Briggs gazed stupidly at Orlando, as if he couldn't grasp the reason for the visit. Orlando pushed the door open further, and stepped inside. Briggs didn't budge, so they were face-to-face, inches apart. Behind him, a middle-aged woman working crochet hooks looked up from a stiff Early American couch. Mrs. Briggs. Orlando hadn't seen her in years. A pre-school boy—a son? No, a grandson—with mouth dropped open, stared from a Lego castle he was building on the floor.

"What are you doing here?" The contempt in Briggs's face almost masked the shamed look of being caught red-handed. Mrs. Briggs let the crochet hooks fall to her lap; her hand cupped her thin mouth.

Orlando could feel Briggs's breath on his face, smell the scent of onions. "Send your wife and the boy from the room." Rage burned within him, but he'd let Briggs save face in front of his wife and the kid. For their sakes, not Briggs's.

"What the—"

"Do it." Orlando shook the bag of cocaine in his pocket.

Briggs looked back into the room and jerked his head. Mrs. Briggs gathered up her yarn and led the little boy from the room.

Briggs let out a snort. "Now, what's this about?"

Orlando pulled the bag from his pocket and

held it in front of Briggs's face. "If I want any more gifts from you, I'll ask. Your little message on my car door was quite enough for this week, thank you."

Briggs shook his head and crossed his arms. "I don't know what you're talking about. Looks like you're in possession of a controlled substance, Orlando."

Flipping the bag upside down, Orlando dumped its contents on the shag carpet, then rubbed it in with his shoe. "It's yours now, Briggs. Better get that vacuumed up before I call the vice squad on you. Hate to have the wife and kid see you dragged off in handcuffs." He stepped out the door, then turned back. "And I don't want to find any more surprises in my car. Or my office. Or my house, for that matter. If I do, I'll come back and break you in half. And I won't show you the courtesy of asking your wife and grandson to leave the room first."

There was a note under his office door. Orlando opened the folded paper wearily. What did the boys have to say this time that they hadn't already scratched in his car door?

But Orlando recognized the handwriting. It was from Bill Shaw, and written on the sergeant's stationery.

Doug,

I'm writing this to clear the air about the other day. I want you to understand my position. I can't afford to come out on your behalf precisely because that kid was black. If the other cops thought I went easy on black hoodlums, I'd lose my credibility in the department. I'm not saying you were wrong in testifying. I'm just saying you shouldn't expect to drag me down with you. I'm sorry about ending our friendship, but that's the way it has to be.

Orlando crushed the letter into a ball and dunked it in the trash. He rounded his desk and, still standing, jotted on a note pad:

Bill,
    Excuses aside, do you really feel good about whose side you're on?

"Do you have the brain of a pea, or what?" Reilly stood with arms crossed in the doorway to Orlando's office. His ears were red, his cheeks puffy with color, his eyes on fire. Behind him, the typewriters of the secretarial center were silent, the area darkened. The typists had gone home for the day. Rain spattered against the window in steady rhythm. "Does stupidity run in your family or did your mother drop you on your head when you were a baby?"

Orlando sat back in his chair. "And I thought you'd be pleased that I found out who bombed that clinic."

Reilly waved a hand. "Luck. Sheer luck. You stumbled onto that one. That's not what I'm talking about, and you know it. We got blacks about to riot because you can't solve this case, and you go running around the city embarrassing the police department." He stepped into the room, his stubby finger jabbing the air. "I told you to lay off Lynch, and you deliberately went against my orders."

Orlando shrugged and picked up a mug on the desk. "I didn't have a lot of choice. I've never let police politics get in the way of justice, and I don't plan to start now." The coffee had gone from steaming to lukewarm. Orlando sipped, shook his head. "If you don't know that already, I'm telling you now."

"And I'm telling you that you're off the case." Reilly gritted his teeth. "I'll make you eat that badge of yours next time you pull a stunt like that."

"I went to Lynch Tower for two reasons. First, Lynch sent one of his henchmen to beat up Donese Jones to keep her quiet—"

"I don't want to hear one more fucking word about that nigger bitch, you hear me? You believe some welfare slut over one of the most respected men in the city."

"I believe the shiner on her cheek."

A cruel grin spread across Reilly's face. "You're really not much of a detective, are you? Ever think of a more likely explanation for that bruise? Like, say, maybe she got in a tussle with our own Detective Orlando when she returned to the scene of the crime? Who says your little melee at the Rabowitz place wasn't with her?" A thick white eyebrow rose questioningly.

"I thought of that," Orlando said flatly. "And I can't say it wasn't." He set the mug down. "But I believe her. I went to see Lynch for another reason, too. He and the rabbi had a secret land deal that went sour. Rabowitz double-crossed him. Lynch could lose out on a deal worth hundreds of millions. That's a reason for murder."

Reilly sighed. "How long you been a cop? Since when do city leaders commit murder?"

"Maybe they don't. But their henchmen do." Orlando leaned back in his chair. "Tell me, what brought all this on?"

"I got a call from the mayor himself. You don't seem to understand who you're dealing with here."

"People keep telling me that." Orlando twisted and pulled the notepad from the pocket of his coat hanging over the back of the chair. He thumbed through the pages. "Now let me see. Ah, here." He picked up the phone and punched out a number. "This is Detective Orlando. You remember me, the one who never has an appointment? I want to speak with your boss."

The secretary gave an annoyed sigh.

"Just tell him I'm on the line. He'll speak with me all right." Orlando looked up to see Reilly shake his head.

"You're digging your own grave, Orlando. I'm gonna have you tarred and feathered for this. Nothing's gonna save you now." The blue eyes twinkled at the thought.

Lynch came on the line with a grunt.

"Lynch," Orlando said into the phone. "This is Detective Orlando. Either you call the mayor and suggest you both butt out of this investigation, or I go straight to Herb Chiligny with the Williamsburg story. If I'm not reassigned to this case in ten minutes, you can kiss your little plan good-bye. I'll also have Donese Jones in your office in an hour to finger the thug who attacked her. What do you think the papers will make of your guard beating her up? And don't count on MacNamara's loyalty. Too many loyal employees have already written bestsellers on their employers' private lives. Don't think MacNamara will go to jail for you. Put that lug under pressure, he'll sing. That's all I've got to say to you. Unless I decide to come over and read you your rights."

Orlando was about to hang up when Lynch said, "Are you finished?"

"Uh-huh."

"First," Lynch said smoothly, "MacNamara who? I know no one of that name. My records show no such person ever working for me. And even though your friend at the *Village World* exemplifies yellow journalism, his editor will still insist on concrete evidence linking me with Rabowitz's land dealings. And you have none. Now good-bye,

Detective Orlando. Good luck on your next assignment." Click.

Orlando slowly set the phone in its cradle. The room seemed suddenly warm.

Reilly just stood there grinning.

CHAPTER 14

It was the hospital where Orlando's father had died. But the years had brought changes. New partitions had sprung up, and bright indirect lighting glowed off aggressively cheery rainbow-striped walls. White tile floors shimmered with wax. Carts in the hallways boasted dinner trays splashed with decorator colors. The whole philosophy of the institution had been altered. Orlando remembered white on white and a businesslike atmosphere. Now it was bustling and festive as a state fair.

Except for the odors. Pine cleaners couldn't hide the smell of illness and death. And the faces. Bright colors couldn't erase the sadness and worry weighing heavily on the faces of visitors to the intensive care unit.

It had been over a decade since he had sat up all night long at his father's side, waiting for the tide to turn. Waiting for the rally that never came. His mother had been there, too, mute, afraid to ask the doctors the prognosis, clutching her rosary beads, silently mouthing a litany of prayer Orlando recognized but had forgotten since abandoning the church so many years before.

Then it was over, the breathing stopped, the waiting ended. The doctor had been kind, speaking softly in words of solace as he walked them to the elevator. On the ride down, Orlando put his arm around his mother, and she buried her face in his chest. He felt the warmth of her tears, but he didn't cry. He was conscious only of numbness, and a resolve for something of which he wasn't sure. It had struck him then that he didn't know whether it was night or day, that hospitals did that to a person. Outside, it was dusk or dawn, the cloud layer thick, rain battering the pavement.

The next day he applied for a transfer to Homicide.

Orlando sighed dolefully. Years had eased the pain, but it was still there, shading his life, and would be until he breathed his last breath.

Ronnie Bell, the medical examiner, stood outside the door to room 221. She stared blankly at the floor, as if its bright shine had caused snow blindness. A leather bomber jacket hung from one fist, the other balled in the pocket of her worn levis. Her faded T-shirt advertised a festival of women's music. The steel-toed boots she wore looked like the kind gay men costumed themselves in back in the seventies when frequenting waterfront bars.

When Orlando spotted her, his eyebrows

knitted together. "You here to see Jennifer Hunt?"

Ronnie looked up and blinked, recognition flooding her face, then confusion. "Huh?"

"Jennifer Hunt. The woman whose hand was blown off at the abortion clinic."

"Yeah." Ronnie tilted her head toward the door. "Her lover is with her now. It's pretty tough. Jen started wailing when they told her about her hand. I don't think I've ever heard a sound so terrible before. They had to put her under sedation." She shook her head bleakly, the fist gripping the jacket tightly, the knuckles white. "So, what brings you here?"

Orlando took off his coat and draped it over his forearm. "I was about to ask you the same question."

Ronnie tensed. The fist came out of the pocket and flattened against her chest. "Me? I've been friends with Stacy and Jen for years. We belong to the same lesbian mothers group. Which reminds me. It's my turn to look after the kids. Sally's in the waiting room with Amy. She's watching Jen and Stacy's son Denny, too. Poor little boy misses his mother, but of course you can't have a two-year-old running around in ICU."

Orlando followed her down the hall. A family huddled by an open doorway. A middle-aged woman twisted a rumpled handkerchief in her hands as tears streamed down her face. An older man with a shock of white hair put his arm around her and murmured reassurances while teenaged boys with long curly hair stared glumly at the floor. The decor of blithe colors seemed a cruel joke when contrasted with the misery in these walls.

"Ronnie, did you know Rabowitz was a suspect in the clinic bombing when I spoke to you Tuesday morning?"

"I didn't know he was a suspect." She looked at him sharply. "I knew he did it. Him and his gang. We all knew it."

"Wouldn't it have been wiser to remove yourself from the case? A suspicious person might think you tampered with the evidence on the body to point away from your friends."

Pale blue eyes, magnified by aviator glasses, locked on Orlando. The voice was hard. "That works both ways. You let a moron like Hennessy do the autopsy, and he could miss evidence that proves Stacy didn't do it. I couldn't take that chance."

Orlando shook his head with exasperation. "And what do you think the medical examiner's office is going to say when they find out?"

"How are they going to know unless you tell them?"

Orlando scowled. "Thanks for making me a party to your questionable ethics." They turned a corner, and a nasal voice over the loudspeaker paged a doctor to the oncology unit. "And was all that bull about respect for the Hasidim's views for my benefit? To throw me off the track?"

A sly grin played on Ronnie's thin lips.

"Well, maybe. But I meant what I said. I hate what Rabowitz did, but I don't hate his corpse. And contacting his wife before doing the autopsy and explaining why it was necessary doesn't seem like too much of an imposition. I have nothing against her. I feel sorry for those women."

The door to the glass-enclosed waiting room was flaming orange. Sally looked up when they entered. Red wavy hair cascaded over the shoulders of her green blouse. She rocked a baby in her arms. A little girl with hair as red and wavy as her mother's sat with legs crossed on the carpet, a storybook in her lap.

Sally wrinkled her nose. "I think Denny just did something."

"I'll take care of it," Ronnie said, digging a diaper from a tote bag on the floor. "Sorry I took so long. Stacy's having a real hard time. Oh, this is Detective Orlando. We work together on a lot of cases." She laid the diaper out on a yellow couch.

Sally released the baby to Ronnie, then threw Orlando a suspicious glance. Denny began to cry, round cheeks rosy. "Now, now, now," Ronnie said, laying him on the couch. "We're going to make you all comfy in a minute." She pulled down little pants and began to work the safety pins. "Don't worry about Orlando. He's one of us. Friend, not foe," she told Sally. "At least I think so." She gave Orlando a narrow eye.

"Well," Sally grunted, "we could use some

friends on the police force. Maybe you could expend a little energy on nabbing the guys who tried to murder Jen."

"Consider it done," Orlando said.

Ronnie balled up the dirty diaper, held it in a raised hand. "Now how to dispose of the evidence of the dastardly act? I know it's not ecologically correct, but I long for the days when we didn't feel guilty about using those disposables. These cloth diapers are for the birds."

"I'll take care of it," Sally said, pushing up from the couch. "I need a walk anyway. Amy, want to make a trip to the bathroom with me?" The little girl nodded, slapped the book shut, and followed her mother, diaper in outstretched hand, out the door.

Ronnie busied herself with the safety pins on the clean diaper. Denny calmed down, cheeks back to normal. "Now, we feel better, don't we?" Denny cooed agreement.

Orlando dropped into an upholstered chair. It was hard, not as friendly as its bright orange fabric promised. "Where were you when Rabowitz was murdered? Here?"

Ronnie picked up the baby, resting him on her shoulder, and walked slowly back and forth. "Yeah. We took turns watching over Jen and going over to the clinic to protect the place." She shot Orlando an indignant look. "Don't tell me I'm a suspect."

Orlando sighed. "No, Ronnie, you're not a

suspect. I've known you too long. But it does bother me that Stacy Black has no alibi."

"Is that why you're here?" Stacy stood in the open doorway. She had aged since he last saw her. Brown eyes carried the weight of pain, circles underneath blue against white skin. Her cheeks were puffy from crying. For the first time Orlando noticed there were gray strands in the frizziness of her long black hair. Her skin was dry and wrinkles cracked at the corners of her mouth. She wore a loose-fitting camel hair sweater and stone-washed jeans. She looked like she had been up all night long, several nights running. "Are you here to arrest me?" There was irony in her voice, but her eyes were dead serious.

"No. Should I be?" Orlando leaned forward. "Actually, I have some news about the bombing. Have you reopened the clinic yet?"

The weary shake of the head showed defeat. "Not yet. We're targeting for Monday." She flopped onto the couch, limp as a rag. "The clinic doesn't seem terribly important to me right now. I've got more important things to attend to." She reached out, and Ronnie put the baby in her arms. "The only reason I want that clinic open as soon as possible is political, and politics are pretty far from my mind at the moment." She hugged the baby, kissed his forehead.

"You can rest assured about one thing. They won't be bombing your clinic again."

She looked up. "Now that their leader is dead, they won't."

"Now that they've all been arrested and confessed, they won't," Orlando said. "You were right. It was Rabowitz and his clan. They used their political meetings as a front for their nighttime forays. Rabowitz didn't realize he was followed by his brother Sunday night when they planted the bomb, and bitter relatives make very good witnesses." Orlando rose, pulled on his coat. "So you can stop worrying about that at least. Your troubles at the clinic are over."

Stacy laughed mirthlessly. "You kidding? The insurance company is balking about paying us a dime. The only reason we're reopening at all is we begged all our friends for whatever money they had saved, and a couple women's groups gave us loans." Denny began to fuss, and she held him to her, rocking gently. "And how do you think I'm going to feel every time I open that door, not knowing what the next moment will bring?"

"You can't give up now. Not when the people who did it are behind bars."

"For how long?" Her voice was fierce, deep. She stroked the baby's silken hair, then looked up at Orlando. "Whatever they do to those people, it won't be enough. Not after what they've done to us. We won't be safe until they're the same place Rabowitz is." She spit out the last word: "Hell!"

*   *   *

Marie Orlando lived down the block from her son in a two-story house with a brick facade painted fire-engine red and mortar painted white. When he'd first seen it, Stewart had commented that it was the most atrocious house on the block, but Orlando thought it fit his mother perfectly. She was from the Old Country, and to her the shiny enamel coating the front of her house was infinitely preferable to the dull brownstones lining the rest of the block. Likewise, the plastic covers on her upholstered furniture seemed not only sensible, but aesthetically pleasing. It kept the fabric like new even though the couch and chairs dated from Orlando's childhood.

Orlando eased onto the lumpy cushions of the couch. The plastic rumpled beneath him. He was tired and achy, too tired to be painting a kitchen this late in the evening. The bump on his head had begun to throb again, and what he really wanted was a good massage from Stewart, something he wouldn't be getting till the damned English tests were graded.

"You sit on my good couch wearing paint clothes?" Marie Orlando's voice was like the chirp of a bird. That is, if chirpy birds had Italian accents. She had met Orlando's father when he was a GI stationed in Rome after the war and been taken with his dark good looks— the result of an Italian mother and a Hispanic father. Marie had returned with him to Brooklyn when his stint in the army was up.

It had not been easy for her, a shy country girl of twenty-three, to leave her family behind and to begin a new life in America. She had been lonely and isolated, despite the large Italian population in her neighborhood. Money was tight and visits back home were rare. She had focused her life on her husband and children, and now that her husband was dead and children grown, she had little to do except spoil her grandchildren whenever she saw them, which was never often enough.

Orlando's father, a mechanic, had scrimped and saved to buy several pieces of property on their block back in the days when houses were cheap. Those investments had left his widow more than comfortable. Still, she continued to wear the same style of ill-cut flowered dresses that she had worn in the fifties, looking more like a lower-middle-class housewife than a woman who owned property in one of the nicer sections of Brooklyn.

"Ma, I'm sitting on the plastic. Isn't that what it's for?"

She nodded, kneading her hands with characteristic worry. "But, Dougie, you get the plastic dirty."

Orlando followed her down a hall. They passed the kitchen. Good smells. Garlic. Green peppers. It had been that way as long as Orlando could remember. They went to the backyard, rummaged through the toolshed for paint, brushes, sandpaper, and a drop cloth, then made their way up the block.

"Who you got moving in?"

"A nice couple." She gave him a nod to show she was impressed. "They're both lawyers."

Orlando had to smile. More yuppies. Marie Orlando opened the door of a basement apartment in a four-story brownstone with a key on a heavy metal ring. They stepped inside and found the light switch. The apartment was roomy, rambling, typical of the houses in the area that had begun their existence at the turn of the century as single-family homes for the wealthy, and had been converted into flats when families became smaller and the need for five-bedroom homes with servants' quarters diminished. The living room was empty, and their footsteps echoed on the hardwood floors.

Orlando set the can of paint on the kitchen counter and pried the lid off. He stirred the paint while his mother inspected the cupboards. "Those boys left this place spotless. Such nice boys." The former tenants had been two gay men who had finally raised the money for a down payment on a condo near Prospect Park.

The neighbor's dog, Gus, began to bark. Orlando groaned as he spread the drop cloth. Marie cupped her hands around her eyes, and peered out the kitchen window into the darkness.

"That dog," she wailed. "I gotta wear earplugs at night because a that dog!"

"Join the club, Ma." He gave the walls and cupboards a quick once over with sandpaper.

Marie paced, a dissatisfied frown on her face. "You can't do something about that dog?"

Orlando sighed. "I'm just a cop. You need a dogcatcher for that monster." He threw the sandpaper aside and dipped a stiff brush into the can of paint. "Or an exorcist." As if in answer, Gus let out a succession of snarls.

Marie paced methodically, lost in thought, stepping carefully on the space between each tile on the imitation brick floor. "I guess I'm just too old," she said. "Too old to live around people and dogs."

Orlando stooped and began to paint the cabinets. A dull ache gripped his lower back. Either it was too late in the evening for this job, or he was just too old himself to work a full day and take care of his mother's property besides.

"Too old to care for alla these buildings by myself," Marie continued.

Orlando stopped in mid-stroke. Warning lights had started to go off. His eyes narrowed, and he gave his mother a searching look. "Okay, Ma. Out with it. What's this all about?"

She waved her hand. "Oh, nothing. It's just that it's been getting to be too much for me, taking care a alla these places. Your father always took care of things when he was alive." She continued to pace, watching her feet fall on the cracks between the tile, but she was obviously glad to have his undivided attention.

"Sell these places," Orlando said. "You'd be rolling in dough."

She shook her head. "No, Dougie. Other than my memories, this is what I have left of your father, God rest his soul." She crossed herself. "He worked his fingers to the bone to buy these buildings, and I'm not gonna give them up. He was right, you know. He said the value of these apartments would just keep going up, and they have. Anyway, this is all I have to leave you and your brother and sister."

Orlando made a sound in his throat. "Ma, we don't need this property. Sell it. Spend your money on yourself. Buy yourself some new clothes. Travel. Go see your sisters in Italy more often. Enjoy yourself. Dad's been gone a long time. You've got to let go. And don't save your money for us kids. You know we're all doing fine."

Pain creased Marie's face, and she stopped pacing. "All but you, Dougie. I worry about you." She looked as if she was going to continue, thought better of it, then tightened her lip.

Orlando set the brush on the paint can and stood. Soreness riddled his thighs. He sighed and wiped his hands on a rag. "C'mon. Tell me what's on your mind."

Her brown eyes teared. "You say I don't get over your father, but you can't either. That's why you do this, this"—she wrung her hands, her face torn with sorrow—"work where they treat you so bad. I'm afraid for you, I'm afraid what'll happen. You're not gonna bring Daddy back, you're not gonna find who killed him. It's been too long."

Orlando rubbed his neck. He was too tired to have this conversation. "You've been talking to Stewart."

She looked guilty, then said, "We only want what's best for you. If you left that place, you could take over for me here. Manage my buildings. Then I travel without having to worry."

Orlando couldn't help but smile. He knew she wouldn't travel any more than she did already. "You're good with an argument, Ma, but that doesn't change the fact that I've always been a cop and always will be."

"Can you think of one good reason to stay?" Her arms were crossed.

He tilted his head. At the moment, he couldn't. Not one. He was too exhausted to think, too worn out to argue. He didn't look at her face. He bent down and resumed painting.

"You can't," she said softly.

Orlando dipped the brush in the paint can, and wiped off the excess. "Let's call a truce, huh? At least until the weekend. We'll talk then. I'm on a tough case, and it's been a rough day."

Motherly concern for his immediate problems superseded her fears about his future. Marie stepped forward, hands still clasped. "You're on that rabbi murder case. With Briggs."

"You *have* been talking to Stewart." He

hadn't bothered to tell anyone he'd been thrown off the case. As far as he was concerned, he was still on it.

"Do you know who did it yet?"

Orlando shook his head. "Not yet. But I'm close. Real close. There are just a few pieces in the puzzle that I can't figure out."

Marie's eyes widened. She was an avid mystery fan, downing mystery novels like an addict swallows pills. Her worry for her son's future seemed left behind. "In Agatha Christie books, you always gotta look for the one with the motive."

"They've all got motives, Ma. Too many motives."

Gus howled next door, but this time Marie ignored him. She raised a finger. "Then opportunity. Look for the person who had the opportunity."

Orlando grinned and dipped the brush in the can. "A lot of them had that, too." But something was bothering him.

"And of course," Marie continued with a faint smile. "It's always gotta be just the last person you would ever suspect."

Orlando was deep in thought. He hardly heard his mother. "That's not the way it works in real life," he said. "At least not usually."

CHAPTER 15

The voice on the phone was vaguely familiar, but she didn't give her name. "Detective Orlando? You awake?" It was Nellie Ridley, a black dispatcher who had furtively called Orlando after the grand jury investigation to thank him for what he had done—she knew showing open support for the detective might jeopardize her job, and she had four kids to raise. This morning, she sounded just as frightened as the last time he had spoken to her a year and a half ago. "We just got a tip that Jimmy Rodriguez is holed up in a shooting gallery on Ashland Place. Detective Briggs is already on the way over there. I thought you should know." She gave the address and hung up, obviously afraid someone was listening over her shoulder.

Orlando blinked at the dead receiver as he lay in bed, then glanced over at Stewart, who had buried his head beneath a pillow when the phone rang. Orlando had been awake for some time; the neighbor's dog had seen to that. Gus had been barking at daybreak. As he set the phone in its cradle, a feeling of disquiet settled in the pit of his stomach. The pieces just didn't fit. Something was missing. The punk Rodriguez might be a part of the solution, but he was not the murderer. Orlando was sure of that. No, the tale behind this killing was more complex than a burglary gone sour. One thing he knew: he had to reach the kid before Briggs did. For the kid's sake, and for the sake of the case. Dead suspects don't talk.

Orlando slipped out of bed, threw on his clothes, packed his Smith & Wesson, grabbed his coat, and stepped out the front door. The cold morning air sent a shiver through him, and he tugged on the coat. The sky looked troubled, patches of blue fighting off an armada of thick gray clouds rolling in on wind currents from the north like an invading navy.

It was colder inside the car. The steering wheel stung his hands. The engine resisted turning over, rumbled, then sputtered to life. The Chevy was pinned between two cars, and Orlando wrestled the wheel back and forth, gently bumping fenders to free the car from its parking space. The streets were deserted, save for an occasional figure, heavily bundled in coat and scarf, briefcase in hand, making for a subway entrance.

A red light stopped him on Smith Street. Ashland Place wasn't that far. Ten minutes. A street of forlorn brownstones and grim warehouses in Fort Greene. A poor and mostly black neighborhood on the fringes of the expensive and white Brooklyn Heights. Fort Greene, where crack houses had sprung up in recent years like lethal weeds whose roots the law could never quite pluck out. Where abandoned buildings became boarded-up shelters for addicts shooting their poison. Orlando tapped his thumbs impatiently on the steering wheel. He wished the sick feeling churning his stomach would go away. Images collided in his head, but brought no answers, only questions. The ghastly face of the dead rabbi, gaping eyes blank. The fragile widow with the tormented eyes. The brother-in-law, so intent on keeping her drugged. What was he afraid she would tell Orlando? The bitter brother and his fellow sect members so intent on revenge. Even with what he now knew, could he totally discount them as suspects? The angry face of Donese Jones swam in his mind. All the black woman wanted was a decent place to raise her kids, but was she willing to kill for it? He thought of Stacy Black at her lover's side in the hospital. She was inflamed enough to kill, but did she? He still had strong suspicions about Lynch, and even Herb Chiligny's vehemence toward the rabbi made Orlando wonder.

The light changed, and he stepped on the gas. Raindrops spattered the windshield as he swung the car down a side street, and he set the wipers to slapping them away. He drove on.

He found the address the dispatcher had
given him, but passed it and parked up the
block. Better not to warn Rodriguez of his arrival. Briggs's Plymouth was nowhere to be
seen. Orlando closed the car door and surveyed the street. It was deserted and silent,
except for the patter of rain on the pavement
and the whistle of the wind. The sky had
clouded over, forcing out the patches of blue,
and the street grew dim. Beat-up cars lined
the curb in front of the sorry brownstones,
some looking better than others, but all dilapidated. Across the street a drab warehouse,
windows painted over, loomed above the abandoned brownstones that bracketed it.

Orlando was relieved Briggs hadn't arrived
yet—he wanted to talk to the kid alone. Without Briggs's heavy-handedness, he might be
able to get to the bottom of this. He took quick
strides down the block, unbuttoning his coat
automatically. Easier to reach for the Smith &
Wesson. He passed squat trash cans overflowing with garbage and rotting smells.

The address was carved in the cement stairs
of the building, which had been ravaged by
fire. From the look of the weathered plywood
covering the windows, held by rusty nails, the
fire must have happened a long time ago.
Flames of soot still reached up from the tops
of the windows, scorching the brick, a record
of the building's demise. The roof had collapsed, taking most of the fourth floor with it,
and jagged beams pointed to the ominous sky.

A derelict sprawled on the stairs. His eyes opened warily at Orlando's approach. The man glanced at a shopping cart set against the building, seemed to decide it was secure enough, and closed his eyes again. The cart was stacked with odds and ends pilfered from garbage cans, probably everything the man owned. Orlando stepped over him. The derelict opened his eyes again, scratched his grizzled beard, and stretched a plaintive palm toward Orlando. Orlando shook his head and pulled aside a two-by-four blocking the open door. Others lay scattered on the grimy linoleum of the hallway.

"Don't go in there," the man said. His face was sunk in, his teeth yellow stubs. He could have been fifty, he could have been eighty. "AIDS."

Orlando looked up when Briggs pulled up in front, double-parking. His heart sank. It would only be more difficult getting what he wanted from Rodriguez now. Briggs got out, slammed the door, and snarled, "What are you doing here?" He pulled two bulletproof vests from his trunk and marched up the stairs with them under his arms, shooting the derelict a scowl of contempt.

Orlando raised his eyebrows. "You didn't bring backup?"

Briggs's eyes were cold. "This baby's mine."

Orlando chuckled sourly. "You want the collar on this case so nobody'll remember your illegal search of the kid's bedroom. You bring in the punk, you get all the publicity for catching the killer and nobody notices your little peccadillo. Smart move, Briggs. I guess you have a stake in Rodriguez being Rabowitz's murderer. Otherwise, you and the department could be in for a hefty lawsuit. And juries have been coming down hard lately on cops who rip innocent people's homes apart."

Briggs threw a vest at him and began strapping on his own. "I'd like to know who tipped you off about this, but I don't really care. I mean, let's face it, with the way Reilly feels about you, who do you think is going to get credit for bringing Rodriguez in?"

Orlando made a face as he put on the vest. "Anybody ever tell you what a swell guy you are?"

"Not lately," Briggs muttered, stepping over the derelict on the stairs.

The man looked up and said, "I wouldn't go in there if I were you. They got AIDS in there."

Briggs scoffed and nudged the man with his shoe. "Get a move on, or I'll lock you up for vagrancy." The man stumbled to his feet, gave Briggs a savage glance, and pulled his shopping cart slowly down the block.

"Now that you've had your little fun, can we get on with this?" Orlando slipped the Smith & Wesson from its holster and watched Briggs do the same. They went inside.

It was dark, but light from the street guided their way. Debris littered the floor, broken bottles and tattered McDonald's bags were strewn about. The doors opening on the hallway were boarded over. Attempts to pry them off had resulted in failure. A staircase marred with graffiti angled upstairs into darkness. Orlando took the stairs with Briggs following behind.

Each stair groaned a mournful lament under their feet, warning of their arrival. Something crunched underfoot, and Orlando peered down to see a syringe crushed under his shoe.

"Nice," Briggs sneered.

The next floor was one large room and as murky as an opium den. It took a moment for Orlando to realize they were not alone. The boards over the windows hadn't succeeded in keeping people out, only light. As his eyes adjusted to the dimness, figures crouched in corners faded in to view. Silent figures, in their own solitary, drug-induced worlds. Some looked up dully. Others didn't bother. Orlando searched the dark forms for the face of Jimmy Rodriguez. No, not on this floor.

The next flight of stairs was missing a banister and blackened by the fire, but sturdy. The light was stronger on the third floor. Someone had yanked the plywood off some of the windows. A man with a glass pipe beside him slumped against the wall. He stared suspiciously. "You cops?"

"We cops," Orlando said.

"Shit. Why can't you people leave us be?"

The man shook his head. His voice was young, but his eyes were old.

"We're looking for Jimmy Rodriguez. You know him?"

"If I tell, you'll leave me alone?"

Orlando nodded.

The man jerked his head toward the staircase. "Up there," he whispered. "He's on the roof."

"The roof" was really the fourth floor of the building since the roof had collapsed into it, bringing down most of the walls. Only parts of the frame of the roof remained, demented iron beams twisted by fire, curling a tortured path above them. A scatter of cold raindrops fell on Orlando's forehead. He looked up. The sky was darkening.

Hunks of tar paper and charred wood obstructed their way. In a corner by the fire escape, a huddled brown mass shivered under ragged blankets. As Orlando and Briggs kicked the debris aside, like explorers breaking through a thicket in a jungle, a head popped out of the blankets.

It was Jimmy Rodriguez. He scowled, scratched his head, and sat up. His hair was greasy, sticking up at wild angles. He still wore the red T-shirt they had seen him in two days before. His face was smudged and his eyes still squinted, this time from the rain.

"You don't look so hot," Orlando said.

Rodriguez eyed their guns and snorted. "No

thanks to you." His nose was red and his voice raspy. He'd been out in the cold too long.

Orlando looked around. "It's not the kind of place I would have run to."

Rodriguez shed the blanket. "I didn't have a lot of choice." He sat on a padding of newspapers. The headlines screamed of Rabowitz's murder. "Who snitched on me?"

"Does it matter?" Briggs said. "We have our contacts."

"Yeah. Snitches."

"Why here?" Orlando stepped closer. "You're not into hard drugs."

The boy shrugged. "I didn't know where else to go. And up here, they leave me alone."

Briggs sighed impatiently and gave Orlando a glance that said it was time to tend to business. "Where were you Monday night? At midnight?"

"I was home. Ask my mom. She'll tell you."

"She already did." Briggs grunted. "She said you were in Puerto Rico. I say you were in Williamsburg cutting up a certain rabbi and ransacking his house for goods."

"I didn't kill him."

"No, you just planted a razor in his neck."

"I didn't do shit," Rodriguez wailed. "I'll take a lie detector test to prove I didn't kill nobody."

"Cut the goddamn bullshit." Briggs breathed heavily. "We found the tools in your closet that you used to break in the back door. Rabowitz fired you for stealing drugs from one of his tenants, and you decided to get revenge by ripping him off."

"I didn't steal nothing from that medicine cabinet," Rodriguez yelled. "That bitch lied. She probably took it herself."

"We've got you on more important offenses," Briggs said. "On Monday night you went over to the Rabowitzes' and cased the joint. You saw the rabbi leave, then Mrs. Rabowitz with the kids. You went around back and checked out the situation there, and when you were sure the neighbors were asleep, you jimmied the back door."

Rodriguez shook his head. "No way, man."

Orlando frowned. He didn't doubt most of what Briggs had said, but he wanted information from the boy, and they weren't going to get it this way. And he had a gut feeling Briggs would do anything to pin the murder on the kid, no matter what the facts said, just to take the heat off his illegal search blunder. "Briggs, ease up."

Briggs dismissed Orlando with the wave of his hand. His eyes burned as he snapped at Rodriguez. "You were in the bedroom rummaging around when you heard footsteps stagger into the bathroom. You knew what would happen if Rabowitz caught you stealing again. You looked for some kind of weapon. Any weapon. And there it was, right on top of the dresser. A brand-new shaving kit, with a shiny sharp straight razor. You grabbed it, Rabowitz walked out of the bathroom and saw the light on in the bedroom. He went to investigate, and there you were. You lunged at him. He picked up the lamp and threw it at you. You scuffled. And then, before he could scream for help, you slashed him so he'd never scream again. And then you ran out the back door. And you didn't even get the loot you came for."

"Hmmm. I guess you got it down pat." Rodriguez rubbed his chin thoughtfully. "Only one problem, you stupid faggot. Can't you read? Didn't the paper say he died from gagging? Someone stuffed some religious shawl down the guy's throat. Now why would I have done that? Think about it."

"You could have done it for any number of reasons." Briggs's jaw remained firm, but his voice betrayed uncertainty. "Don't tell me you weren't there."

Rodriguez shrugged. He rose to his feet, stretching his arms. "Oh, I was there all right. But I didn't kill nobody."

"We'll let a jury decide that."

Rodriguez stared at him. "You're fucked. You don't even care who really did it." He shot a quick glance behind him, then bolted for the fire escape. He scrambled over rotting debris and dove onto the fire escape, which swayed under his weight. Pinions gripping it to the wall creaked. Rodriguez disappeared two steps at a time.

"I'll follow him," Briggs yelled. "You go down the stairs. We'll trap him in the alley."

Orlando started for the stairs, stopped. "Briggs! I want that kid alive, hear?"

Briggs climbed onto the fire escape, turned, said, "Don't worry about it." There was a glint in his eye. And then he was gone.

Orlando stormed down the steps, cursing himself all the way. The planks beneath his feet protested with sharp accusations. He should have seen it coming. He should have taken charge of the interrogation. Hell, he should have gotten rid of Briggs and talked to the boy alone. Rodriguez might not know who killed the rabbi, but he was the last person to see him alive before the murderer struck. And something told Orlando that if the punk was offered immunity for the burglary attempt, he might have a good idea of who the murderer was. Maybe Rodriguez was still in the house when the killer showed up.

As Orlando rounded the stairs on the second floor, footfalls like thunder, addicts looked up in stupefied slow motion. Orlando took the last flight and raced out into the rain. He looked both ways, then cornered the building. The fire escape shook with violence. Rodriguez leapt down the steps, catapulting himself from landing to landing, arms waving frantically. Briggs stomped down behind him, gun raised, shouting, "Stop you little motherfucker or I'll shoot."

Rodriguez jumped from the fire escape to the brick-paved alleyway, landing on his knees. He stumbled to his feet, stared at Orlando standing before him, then hobbled the other way like a crippled racehorse about to be put out of its misery. He wasn't going anywhere fast.

Orlando headed after him. "Hold it, Rodriguez. Make it easier on yourself. You can't get away."

"Orlando! Stand back!" Briggs hollered. He crouched in firing position on the last landing of the fire escape.

Orlando heard the pistol cock. *Oh, no, not again,* his mind screamed. Everything went in slow motion. *Briggs's grimacing face as he pulled the trigger. The hollow report of the Smith & Wesson again and again. The sledgehammer force thrusting Rodriguez face first into the pavement. The ever-widening circles of crimson on the kid's back.*

Orlando trotted over to Rodriguez, holstered his gun, crouched, turned him over, and rested the boy's head in his hands. Rodriguez looked up at him stupidly. A drop of blood hovered on his lower lip. Scratches etched his cheeks.

"I didn't do it," the youth whispered.

"I know," Orlando said. "Do you know who did?" He looked up to see Briggs jump down from the fire escape and land heavily.

Rodriguez struggled for air. "I donno. I didn't mean to hurt Rabowitz. It's just that he came home when I was robbing the place. He jumped on me. I had to protect myself." His eyes began to glaze over. He was seeing things Orlando couldn't see.

"Then what, Rodriguez? What happened then?"

"Someone came in. The front door. And I ran." The eyelids flickered and the body went limp.

Briggs strolled up. "Did he confess?"

Orlando felt the neck for pulse. None. Too late for an ambulance now. He laid the head gently on the ground, wiped his hands, and rose. A burning sensation gripped his stomach, that commotion in his gut he had felt so many times in the last year and a half.

"No," he said quietly. *Stay calm, keep the fire contained, don't show how you feel.* "He didn't confess. He admitted slashing the rabbi, but we already suspected that. He said someone came in the front door, so he ran."

Briggs scoffed. "Still trying to cover his tracks. The kid was guilty." He gave Orlando a tentative grin. "You'd make it easier on the both of us if you said he confessed just before dying."

"Easier for you. You didn't have to shoot him."

The grin died. "The punk was a felony suspect running from the police. He was a danger to the public."

"You did it to save your own neck, and you know it." *Don't show your anger*, the voice within told him. But this time Orlando had to ask himself, *Why not?*

Briggs stripped off the vest, secured his gun in its holster, and buttoned his coat. He held the vest under his arm. "I don't care what you think, and don't go making trouble. I know what happened here. I went after Rabowitz's killer, and I got my man."

"Yeah," Orlando said. "But it was the wrong one. You're not getting away with this." His fist clenched, hard as stone.

Briggs shrugged. "I don't know why not. I did before."

I did before. There was something about the way he said it, the confident tone, the casual air. It was like dropping gasoline on the flames scorching Orlando's gut, and he exploded inside. All the rage that burned within him surfaced: the harassment he had endured, the frustrating humiliations that had become a part of his daily life, the damage this whole mess had done to his relationship with Stewart, and especially, the slumped forms of not one, but two boys shot in the back. For a fragment of a second, Orlando went a little mad.

Orlando shot out a fist that knocked Briggs backward, a blow that was meant to kill. Stumbling, wind knocked out of him, face red with fury, Briggs reached for his gun. Orlando landed a foot in his groin, heard a gasp as it hit its mark, then pummeled his face in a staccato blur of fists. Briggs staggered, hands clutching his groin, then plopped heavily on his butt on the pavement. His face, swollen, was smeared with blood from his torn lower lip. When his mouth sagged open, Orlando saw his teeth were stained red.

"You fucking maniac!" Briggs spit out blood. He yanked his gun from its holster and pointed it at Orlando.

Orlando shook his head gravely. "You don't have the guts. Shooting a punk in the back, yeah. But try to justify killing a cop."

Briggs faltered, let the gun hang. He breathed in heaving gasps. Finally, he said, "It doesn't have to be me. Someday, every cop needs a backup. And the men of the force aren't going to be there when you need them. You just wait, Orlando. I don't have to be the one to do it. Someday, you'll get yours."

"Not before I bring you down first." Orlando spat on the pavement, then turned on his heel and walked away.

CHAPTER 16

The window of Orlando's office overlooked the wide front steps of the station house. A strong wind had carried in a thick blanket of clouds, but the rain had stopped and the day had brightened. A throng of reporters surrounded Lieutenant Reilly. His thinning white hair, combed for the occasion moments before, was already disheveled, and his trench coat flapped in the breeze.

It had been a good week for the lieutenant. The day before he had announced the arrest and confessions of the men who bombed the abortion clinic, and now he was about to announce the capture and death of the murderer of Rabbi Avraham Rabowitz. His face, cheeks brushed with color, shone with pleasure. Television cameras whirred, flashbulbs shot out white light.

Orlando stood watching silently through venetian blinds parted by his hand. He stared down at the pantomime below, his face expressionless. The only sound was the whisper of the wind against the dirty panes. Reilly waved his hands proudly, then stuck out his chest like a bantam rooster. Then Briggs, face puffy and bruised, appeared by his side, flashbulbs exploded like so many firecrackers of light, and microphones were thrust forward. Reilly placed his arm around Briggs's shoulder.

Orlando turned away and let the blinds snap back into place. He wandered his small office, kneading his chin thoughtfully. He hadn't had time to shave that morning, and his face was scratchy—the way Stewart liked it. Well, maybe tonight. After all, it was the end of test week.

Orlando sighed glumly. Today marked the end of a lot of things. The end of the case. The end of a fifteen-year-old's life in a dirty alley behind a shooting gallery. He reached over to a mug on his desk and took a sip. The coffee was cold. He swallowed with distaste, set the mug down, and stared at the neat piles of paper on the blotter. Mrs. Burdict had been tidying up. The land options, the receipts from the antique shop, Rabowitz's police file, the stack of newspaper articles on the rabbi. They were meaningless now, as meaningless as the deaths of Jimmy Rodriguez and the black punk a year and a half ago, and that made him mad. All week long he'd been looking in the wrong direction for the killer.

He flung the papers off the desk. They scattered on the floor in a jumbled heap. The mug toppled, spilling a puddle of brown on the blotter. Coffee dripped from his sleeve, and he pulled a handkerchief from his pocket and wiped it dry.

He grunted. Well, at least he had a reason to stay now. All week long he'd been prodded by all sides to quit; every day he'd searched for one reason to continue. And he hadn't found one. Until now. The killing of the Rodriguez boy made it painfully clear to him.

Other than Orlando, who was there to stand up against the Briggses on the force? Who was there to say *no* to the corruption rotting the department? Maybe he couldn't beat them, but at least he was there, fighting against the inequities of the system.

He thought about what Stewart had said the other evening. Yes, he had transferred into Homicide years ago in reaction to his father's unsolved murder, bowing to a gut desire to avenge his death. But that wasn't why he was here today. He stayed because he was needed, and that was reason enough. He wasn't going to leave because of Briggs's actions or what Reilly did to him. He would remain, and cops like Reilly and Briggs made it all the more important that men like Orlando were on the force. Maybe there weren't enough of his kind to provide checks and balances against bad cops, but at least it was something. All he knew was that he would stick it out till retirement.

And he had a score to settle with Briggs. Smashing up his face provided only temporary satisfaction.

He paced by the window, paused, and like a driver slowing down to see a traffic accident, pulled up the blinds and stared bleakly at the assemblage on the steps. The press conference was as disturbing to him as a car wreck and just as ugly. He wondered what Mrs. Rodriguez was doing right now. Probably shielding her aging mother from the news. Their telephone would be ringing off the hook, and reporters beating on their door. Orlando drew a deep breath. The crowd was dispersing now. They had got what they wanted: their story for the evening news, their sound bites, their pictures. Reilly and Briggs disappeared into the front of the station house, grinning. Everybody had got what they wanted.

But maybe Orlando could have what he wanted, too. He wouldn't know until this evening, but he figured Briggs might have just dug his own grave.

Orlando let the blinds drop, but continued to stare out the window through the slats. He had spent the morning pondering what his mother had told him the night before in her silly advice culled from Agatha Christie books. And finally he'd understood why her words had weighed on him; he knew who the killer was. But too late to save Jimmy Rodriguez's life. Sure the kid was guilty, too, but he wasn't alone. The truth had been staring him in the face all along, but he'd been too absorbed with the bizarre aspects of the case to see how simple the murder really was.

He grabbed his coat. It was time to bring the killer in.

Orlando stopped at the top of the main stairway of the station house. Below, several uniforms gathered around Reilly and Briggs, backslapping, boisterous. He couldn't hear the words, only a jumble of sounds, but what he saw made him sick inside. Orlando spotted Bill Shaw speaking quietly with the desk sergeant on the side of the room.

Briggs broke from the crowd and strolled over to Shaw, placing a friendly hand on the black man's shoulder. Shaw shook Briggs's hand off, gave him a cold stare, then turned away. As he did, his eye caught Orlando's at the top of the stairs. He gave Orlando a nod, then turned back to the desk sergeant and continued his conversation. Briggs stood there with a perplexed expression on his face.

Orlando wasn't sure what had just happened, but he thought he had just witnessed the tide beginning to turn.

The boys were playing in the tiny cemented-over yard, fenced by wrought iron painted shiny black. One tall, gangly, with stringy blond hair and a loose T-shirt and torn jeans, the other short and roly-poly in a puffy down coat. It was midday, and the sun had broken through the cloud layer, bringing with it a checkerboard of blue sky. The wind whipped down the street, singing through naked tree branches, snatching up bits of litter and grit, and casting them in the air like a hand sowing seed. The boys didn't hear Orlando approach.

"You have to throw it harder, Yakov," David said. He threw a ball against the side of the brownstone. "Like this."

The little boy tried to catch the oversized ball on the rebound, missed, and toppled on the cement. When he looked about to cry, the older boy scolded, "You're all right. You just got to be quicker." Yakov struggled to his feet.

"I think you need a smaller ball," Orlando said. "That one's about as big as he is."

David spun around, brushing blond locks out of his eyes with a scabby hand, and stared suspiciously at Orlando with the wariness of a child brought up in the big city. Recognition spread over his face, but the distrust remained. He picked up the ball and put his arm around the little boy. "You're one of the cops who visited my dad a couple mornings ago."

Orlando read his watch. "I thought you were so intent on being in school. Surely it's not out yet."

David shrugged. "They wanted me to stay here and play with Aunt Sarah's kids. I don't know how they expect me to pass math this quarter when they don't let me go to class."

He didn't look the type who would be interested in math to Orlando. "I'm sure you'll do fine."

"Just tell that to my math teacher." He pounded the ball on the pavement with hard thrusts, then looked up again. "I guess you know they got the guy who killed my uncle. Shot him down in an alley. I'm glad it happened that way. Now we don't have to put up with the snoopy press during a trial. I'm sick of them coming around. The kid deserved it anyway."

"I was there," Orlando said. "He didn't deserve what he got."

Orlando climbed up the stairs and rapped on the door. After a moment, Michael Greenberg opened it. "Oh," he said. "It's you. I thought it would be another reporter. I didn't know they had so many in this town. Now that they got the guy who did it, maybe we'll get some peace. I'll tell you frankly, I'm glad this is all over with."

"It's not over with." Orlando brushed by him into the house.

Anna Greenberg reclined in an easy chair in the living room. A three-year-old lay in her lap, a storybook opened in her hands. Orlando recognized the child from the picture on Mrs. Rabowitz's mantelpiece. The room was bathed in soft light from the front windows, but the lamp also shone at her side. She looked up, lifted reading glasses from her nose, and said, "Michael, take Detective Orlando's coat." Her brown eyes said she wasn't glad to see him.

Orlando handed his coat to Greenberg, and he hung it in the hall closet. Anna set the book aside and rose with the child in her arms. "I'll

leave you men to talk. It's time for Morde-
chai's nap anyway."

"I would like you here." Orlando sank into
the couch. "Please come back after you've put
the baby to bed. And bring Mrs. Rabowitz."

Anna's face tightened, but she nodded as
she slipped out of the room. Greenberg forced
a smile, but his gray eyes betrayed uneasiness.
He scratched the peach fuzz on his balding
head and said in a tone meant to be jocular,
"How about a drink? I take it you're off duty
now that the case is over." He crossed to a
cabinet of teak, opening its doors. Glasses
tinkled.

"No thanks. I'm still on duty."

Greenberg turned. "Well, I hope you won't
mind if I indulge. Even we doctors have our
vices." When he poured, the bottle of bourbon
clinked repeatedly against the crystal glass.

"So," Greenberg said, taking a sip. "I suppose you're here to officially inform us that
Rodriguez was captured for Avraham's murder, and uh, killed trying to escape. Actually,
someone dropped by earlier from the police
department to tell us, although by that time a
dozen reporters had beaten him to it."

"That's not why I'm here."

"Oh." His fleshy face fell, and he gulped
more bourbon. At the window, he gazed down
at the boys playing. "That son of mine."
Greenberg shook his head. "Doesn't look like
me, talk like me, think like me. When I was
his age, I already knew what I wanted to be.

I was enrolled in college prep courses and president of my class. I don't understand how he could be so different. All he wants to do is listen to that terrible music."

"Kids have a tendency to do that to you," Orlando grunted.

"I'm not complaining," Greenberg said quickly, "considering how some brats turn out. Look at that Rodriguez kid. Think of how his mother must be feeling."

"I have been. All afternoon. I keep remembering it was you who gave us the lead to investigate Rodriguez. Same with Menachem Rabowitz. You pointed me in his direction the night of the murder. At first I thought you were just being helpful."

"At first?" Greenberg's eyes narrowed.

"At first. I don't think that anymore."

"And what's that supposed to mean?" He said it stiffly, knocking back the last of the bourbon in his glass.

"Coffee?" Anna stood in the doorway holding a tray of cups and saucers and a coffeepot. It took a moment for Orlando to realize that she wasn't alone. Mrs. Rabowitz was behind her, silent. Anna breezed into the room, placing the tray on the coffee table. "You want a cup, don't you, Detective Orlando? This is a blend I'm sure you'll enjoy. I got it at a little Italian shop just down the street that has so many wonderful kinds."

She was all genteel hostess, talkative and bright. As she poured a cup, she said, "How about you dear? You look like you could use some good coffee." Greenberg nodded dully. "And you Sarah," she continued, "why don't you sit right there. You still need your rest." Mrs. Rabowitz sat in the easy chair. "Isn't Sarah looking better, Detective Orlando?"

Sarah Rabowitz's tiny figure was enveloped by the cushions of the recliner, giving her the appearance of a child set in too large a chair. Her hair was styled simply, her sad eyes, creased with dark circles, clear and watchful. Her blouse was black, ill-fitting, with a cascade of ruffles down the front and a high collar of lace.

"Yes, now that your husband isn't pumping dope into her." Orlando reached over and took a cup and saucer. "You know, for a while I thought he was trying to keep her from telling me what she knew." Steam rolled from the cup as he sipped the full-bodied brew. "That is good. You'll have to tell me what it's called. I will say one thing though, Mrs. Rabowitz, the blouse doesn't do you justice."

"Oh, that's mine," Anna said. She brought her husband a cup and saucer. "All her things are still at her house. It was the only thing I had in black."

"Really? I doubt that. But it does a good job of covering the bruises."

Anna froze, her hands still gripping the saucer she had handed to her husband. Greenberg glared, his eyes darkening. Mrs. Rabowitz sighed with resignation. "How did you know?" Her voice was stronger than it had been, but carried a fragile quality, like the ring of a glass bell.

Orlando shrugged. "You always have your neck covered. You had a scarf tied around your neck the night of the murder. Hasidic women wear scarves on their heads, not around their necks. Then when I visited you here on Wednesday, you kept a blanket wrapped around your neck. I'd been told about the statistics of wife beating in the Hasidic community. It just took me a while to put two and two together. I guess I just didn't want to believe you did it."

"This is ridiculous," Greenberg scoffed. "The police department says Jimmy Rodriguez killed Avraham. Where do you get off saying otherwise?"

"Oh, he cut up the rabbi, all right, but Rabowitz didn't die of razor wounds. He died from being smothered with a prayer shawl. That's the piece of the puzzle that didn't fit. Why wouldn't Rodriguez have just taken another swipe with the razor if he wanted to kill him?"

Anna crouched by her sister, grasping her birdlike hands. "Why can't you leave things alone," she whined. "Haven't we suffered enough? Leave it alone. Let Sarah raise her kids in peace."

Orlando looked at Anna Greenberg sadly. "I can't do that. This isn't a simple murder case anymore. It's become bigger than that. If people think some Hispanic kid murdered the rabbi, we'll just see more violence between minorities. I have to tell the truth."

Greenberg threw Orlando a savage glare. "Having bruises on your neck doesn't prove you're a murderer."

"No, not in itself, of course. I first began to wonder when I saw the checkbook and the bankbook on the bedside table the night Rabowitz was killed. By the phone where Mrs. Rabowitz called the police. It didn't seem important at the time, but the rabbi kept all that sort of stuff in the rolltop desk in the living room.

"The blood spot on the light switch in the dining room bothered me, too—Mrs. Rabowitz told me she always left that light on to fool burglars when she wasn't home. If that was the case, why would the rabbi have had to touch it?

"Also, Mrs. Rabowitz, you took the kids to visit your sister so late at night—how many mothers bring their young children on a visit after eight-thirty at night? And then there was the closet. It was only half full, and all the clothes were the rabbi's. Black trousers, suit jackets, white shirts."

"I'm sure you're mistaken," Greenberg said quickly. He tasted the coffee and nodded with satisfaction. "I suggest you check again."

"Four cops saw what was in that closet, and there wasn't a stitch of Mrs. Rabowitz's clothes. I dropped by earlier this afternoon"—

he dug in his pocket and dangled a set of keys—"and dresses were hanging in the closet. As a matter of fact, they were there Tuesday night when I was hit on the head, but I was preoccupied looking for an intruder and didn't notice. Obviously someone put them there. I found it strange that you didn't want to change your dress Monday night, Mrs. Rabowitz—it had your husband's blood on it, after all. You said you just wanted to come here to your sister's and be with your children as quickly as possible. Now I see the reason was you had nothing at your house to change into."

"This is absurd!" Greenberg cried. He set the cup and saucer on the lamp table, and stood behind Mrs. Rabowitz's chair. He placed firm hands on her shoulders.

Orlando stuffed the keys in his pocket. "By the way, Dr. Greenberg, I want you to know that it's a crime to strike a police officer on the head. I take it you used a suitcase." His eyebrow rose questioningly, and he felt the back of his head. "A heavy metal suitcase."

Greenberg shook his head and raised his hands in exasperation. "I'm afraid you've totally lost me."

"You knew that eventually the police would notice that all of Mrs. Rabowitz's clothes and all of the children's were missing. Questions would be asked. So on Tuesday night you convinced Mrs. Rabowitz to give you the key. You packed some of their clothes in a couple of suitcases and sneaked in the back door. After

you put her clothes back and were in the boys'
room about to do the same, you heard someone
come in the front door. Me. And when I inves-
tigated, you bashed me on the head, dumped
the clothes in the room, and ran out back with
the suitcases."

"Before you said the room had been ransacked. That someone was looking for something. Why don't you make up your mind?"

"I was wrong. All the drawers were neatly
closed. Why would an intruder ransacking the
place and throwing clothes around close the
drawers?"

"This is not evidence of anything!" Greenberg
snorted. "You call yourself a detective?
Where's your concrete proof?"

Orlando set the cup and saucer on the coffee
table and sat back. "We could check with the
phone company," he offered. "I think they'll
have a record of a phone call from the Rabowitz residence to yours at about midnight on
Monday. Mrs. Rabowitz, when you called Dr.
Greenberg in my presence the night of the
murder, you told him that the rabbi had been
murdered, but that was all for show, wasn't
it? He was already well aware that you had
killed your husband."

Mrs. Rabowitz's eyes wavered, filled with
tears. "Enough," she said quietly. She freed
one hand from her sister's grasp and reached
up and gripped Greenberg's. "I've gotten you
in enough trouble already. It's time to tell the
truth. Too many people have been hurt." She

gave them both a look of gratitude, then addressed Orlando. "My husband was not a kind man, Detective Orlando."

Orlando nodded. "I got that idea somewhere along the line."

She pulled away from Anna and Greenberg, and touched her neck. "This wasn't the first time he beat me, and I knew it wouldn't be the last." She shook her head, and tears rolled down her cheeks. "I was so ashamed. He would hit me in front of the children. I would refuse to go out until the bruises healed. Sometimes I was lucky, and he would hit me where it wouldn't show. My arms. My stomach.

"Anna and Michael begged me to leave him. I knew they were right, but I couldn't. I was afraid of Avraham. He could be so vindictive. Look at what happened when he left his old synagogue. Once when I threatened to leave him, he said he'd get custody of the children even if he had to pay people to lie in court. He said he'd have me found an unfit mother. That he'd turn my children against me."

She drew a long breath and wiped her eyes. "And I felt like an unfit mother. Worthless. I could have taken the beatings, but I kept thinking of the children. I had to save them from seeing that." She paused and stared blankly at the floor. "And I had stopped believing. Believing in God, in the rituals we lived by. I decided that's not how I want my kids raised, not with the weight of tradition burdening them all the time."

"Go on," Orlando said gently.

"He came home angry Monday evening. Dinner wasn't ready, and the table hadn't been set, and he—" she faltered, put her palms to her face, then regained her composure. "He slapped me and grabbed me around the neck. I was gasping for breath and blue in the face by the time he let me go. I vowed then I would leave him for good. After he left for his meeting, I packed my things and the kids' stuff. I brought the car around to the alley to load the suitcases. I didn't want the neighbors gossiping. Anna and Michael were so happy to see us on their doorstep. They said they knew a lawyer who could see me the next morning about the divorce. Once we were settled in, Michael mentioned that there were things I should have to give to the lawyer. Bank account numbers so that our assets could be frozen so Avraham didn't plunder them before the divorce went through and so on. They offered to accompany me home. I think Anna was afraid I would break down and return to Avraham if he put me under the slightest pressure. But I was sure he wouldn't be home yet—his meetings lasted late into the night—and I told them it was better if I went alone."

The front door burst open, bringing with it a gust of wind. David bounced the ball on the hallway floor. Yakov ran to his mother. She wrapped her arms tightly around him.

"It's getting too cold for Yakov," David said. "School will be out soon. I'm gonna spend some time with the guys." Then he was gone, the door slamming behind him.

Mrs. Rabowitz flipped off the boy's hood and stroked his shaved head. "Did you have fun, honey?"

"Yes," Yakov said. "But the ball was too big."

"Why don't you take off your coat and go to the playroom, okay?"

Yakov disappeared out the arched doorway of the living room, and his footsteps echoed downstairs. Mrs. Rabowitz watched him go, her face pained.

"Go ahead," Orlando said.

"When I got home, I went straight for the rolltop desk. It wasn't until I had the bankbook and the checkbook in my hand that I realized something was wrong. The light in the dining room was on. Even though I usually left it on when I wasn't home, I hadn't bothered that night—why should I? I hadn't planned to ever come back. Then I saw the blood splotch on the light switch and the light streaming from the bedroom down the hall. I stood there, deathly still. And then I heard footsteps running out back. I stood frozen for a full minute, not knowing what I would find in the bedroom ..."

A tear ran down her cheek, and she lapsed into silence.

"You walked in," Orlando prodded, "and he lay there helpless in a pool of blood. I can just imagine what his eyes looked like. Hopeful at first when you appeared in the doorway, then changing to befuddlement when you didn't rush to the phone to call for help. Then to surprise and horror as you knelt over him and stuffed that thing down his throat as he gasped and gagged."

Mrs. Rabowitz put her face in her hands and shook in silent sobs. Then calmness came over her and she looked up, her eyes red, plaintive. "It wasn't like that. When I saw him, I rushed to the phone by the bed. I put the checkbook and the bankbook down and began to call for an ambulance."

"But you stopped."

She nodded. "I knew if I called an ambulance, he might live. Now that I was back in that house, I knew he would never let me go. That I would be chained to him for life. I watched him gurgling up blood. I thought, if I just wait a minute, maybe ... But no, I realized he might live and tell that I had refused to call for help. I knew what I had to do. I saw the razor lying there, bloody, glistening in the light. But I couldn't bear to touch it. And of course if I did, it would leave fingerprints. Then I saw the prayer shawl lying among the things thrown around the room. I grabbed it in a frenzy and stuffed it down his throat. It was as if I was saving myself. He didn't struggle; he was too weak. It took him several minutes to die. I watched as his eyes glazed over. Then I called Anna and Michael, and told them what I had done."

"Sarah wanted to go to the police," Greenberg said glumly. "It was my idea to cover the whole thing up. We agreed to lie about the time Sarah left our house, to pretend she was just visiting and the kids had fallen asleep."

"I called the police, but it wasn't until they knocked on the front door that I remembered the bruises on my neck," Sarah said quietly. "I took the kerchief from my head and used it to cover them."

Orlando leaned forward and poured himself another cup of coffee. "And you kept her drugged as much as possible to keep the police from questioning her, finding holes in her story."

Michael Greenberg nodded sadly. "We love Sarah and would do anything to protect her and the kids."

The little boy, shorn of his coat but still roly-poly, waddled into the room and to his mother's side. He clutched a silver toy airplane.

"Is Daddy going to Heaven?" he asked. He drove the airplane down his mother's leg.

Mrs. Rabowitz pulled him to her lap, and rocked gently back and forth. "No, dear. That's all superstition. When you die, you die. That's it. That's why it's so important to do everything you want while you're alive, to live life to the fullest ..." She wrapped her arms around him and held his head to her breast. She stroked his hair and kissed him on the forehead.

It wasn't until she began to shake that Orlando knew she was crying.

CHAPTER 17

Poindexter moaned a long lugubrious sigh to the strains of Rimsky-Korsakov's *Scheherazade*. His eyes, already sad, seemed about to weep to the lone violin. Then he blinked thoughtfully, grunted, and nuzzled his nose into Orlando's stockinged feet. The dog's tail patted the carpet. This was Poindexter's way of saying that he was ready for his late-night walk.

"Do you really need to go?" Orlando demanded. He reclined in the easy chair, his body sunk in its thick cushions. He didn't want to move. He ached all over, as much from the tension of the week as from his scuffle Tuesday night at the Rabowitz place. He touched the bump on his head. Still there, but going down, no longer throbbing. He reached over, took a last swig from a bottle of seltzer on the table, and looked Poindexter in the eye.

Poindexter glanced away guiltily, then met his gaze. The tail went between his legs. The eyes turned melancholy.

Orlando slapped the armrest and pushed up

heavily. "You win. I can't stand it when you look at me with those eyes."

He reached over and turned off the compact disc player. The house was quiet. Stewart had gone to bed an hour earlier. The tests were all graded, the semester over. Orlando had suggested celebrating, in bed, but Stewart begged off until tomorrow, pleading exhaustion.

Poindexter's tail thumped the carpet with the precision of a metronome. He knew what was coming. Orlando wrestled into his shoes, hunted the leash, and clicked it on Poindexter's collar. The basset led him to the door, and Orlando pulled on his jacket from the hall closet as he shut the front door behind him.

The night was hard and cold. The winds of the evening had swept the clouds away, and icy stars stared down from a black heaven. Naked tree branches rustled in the breeze. Orlando's footsteps, hollow on the crooked cement slabs of the sidewalk, and the click of Poindexter's nails as he trotted along, sniffing at tree trunks, were the only signs of life on the street.

But spring was just around the corner. Orlando could smell it in the briskness in the air. Leaves would be sprouting on the tree-lined street, bringing color to the brick and sandstone and concrete. The window boxes would fill with reds, yellows, blues.

The thought renewed him, despite his weariness. Good things were to come, he decided. And part of that was staying on with the department, no matter the difficulties. He had weathered troubled times before, he could do it again. He was needed, and that was what mattered. When he had explained this to Stewart that evening, the words came out jumbled, sounding silly. Stewart hadn't seemed impressed with his logic, but reached over and gave him a firm hug.

"I married a cop, so I guess it's my fate to worry like a cop's wife. You have to admit, I haven't hounded you to quit in"—he regarded his watch—"over seventy-two hours. But don't expect miracles. I love you too much not to nag now and then." With that, Stewart planted a kiss on his forehead and slipped off to bed.

Poindexter tugged on his leash, snorted feverishly at a tree trunk, and did his business. They walked on. The streetlights shone silver on the sidewalk. A howling arose over the neighborhood. Gus, the neighbor's dog, doing what he did best. Orlando shook his head. It was going to be another sleepless night on the block.

They stopped at the corner. "You done?" Poindexter looked satisfied, licked at Orlando's heels, and they turned toward home.

Orlando thought about Mrs. Rabowitz. He wondered what would become of her. Sometimes the courts went lightly on women like that, mothers of small children who were victims of abuse. But not always. Even a couple of years away from her children would be a terrible punishment, both for her and the kids.

At least she had a family who could take them in.

Reilly had not been happy with the outcome of the case. After his press conference announcing Rodriguez as the killer, it made him appear somewhat foolish to call a second conference a few hours later to explain what really happened. The evening news had said that Briggs could not be reached for comment.

Orlando wasn't sure if there would be a grand jury investigation of the Rodriguez shooting. But if there was, he'd be there to testify. If he was going to stay on, he'd better get used to being lonely. But then again, maybe that wasn't so. Bill Shaw's snub of Briggs this afternoon might signal the beginning of a change in how Orlando was treated in the department.

He had called Donese Jones after he heard she'd dropped her assault complaint. He tried to convince her to reinstate it, but she was afraid of what Lynch might do next if she persisted. And she had no faith in the judicial system. "Nothing going to be done anyway." Orlando, however, promised himself that something was going to be done. Maybe Lynch could get away with hurting poor women, but Orlando could strike back with ruthless force. Tomorrow he would call Herb Chiligny and give him an exclusive on the Williamsburg land deal. Even though there was no paper evidence linking Lynch to Rabowitz, Orlando would be a reliable enough source to convince

Chiligny's editor to print the story. After all,
Lynch had admitted the whole thing to him.
If nothing else, it might keep some low-income
people in affordable housing rather than out
in the street.

And Chiligny would be getting another exclusive, too. Briggs had let his ego run away
with him—he couldn't admit that a gay man
had busted up his face. He'd said at the press
conference that the bruises on his face were
the result of Rodriguez attacking him and
that the shooting was in self-defense—a claim
that could easily be proved false by a medical
examiner's investigation. It was ironic that
shooting an unarmed man wasn't grounds for
kicking Briggs out of the department, but lying
to the press—and falsifying his police report—
just might be. The *Village World* knew how to
make a big stink; maybe, just maybe, Briggs's
days on the force were numbered.

An article in the midsection of the evening
paper announced the disbanding of the neighborhood patrol in Williamsburg, along with
guarded exclamations of brotherly love from
both the Reverend Melvin Packard and leaders of the Jewish community. But Orlando
noted the patrol had disbanded rather than integrate, and knew only a tenuous truce had
been forged.

Orlando climbed the stairs to his apartment
and fitted the key in the lock. When he opened
the door, warm air rushed at him. He freed

Poindexter, took off his coat, and hung it in the closet.

It was time for bed. Poindexter wrapped himself in a ball in a padded wicker basket in the corner of the living room. Orlando switched off the lamp and made his way to the bedroom.

Stewart breathed slowly and evenly in the darkness. Orlando pulled off his shoes and set them on the floor. He shed his clothes and stood over the bed. He felt arousal tingle in his thighs. He bit his lip. Tomorrow. Stewart had said tomorrow. Orlando grimaced, sighed, and silently slipped into bed.

He gently wrapped his arms around Stewart from behind, felt the warmth of his smooth taut body sink into him, felt the perfect fit as they lay like one under the comforter.

Then Gus let out a yap and a growl from the neighbor's yard.

Stewart shifted, murmured in his sleep, pressed closer to Orlando.

Gus snarled, let out a staccato series of re-sounding barks.

Stewart's body tensed. He lifted his head. His voice was a whisper. "That dog keeps waking me up."

Orlando gripped him tighter. "You know," he said. "It's after midnight. It *is* tomorrow." Stewart sat up, turned toward him. He felt Stewart's soft chest hair against his. A hand slid down his thigh. Orlando covered Stewart's lips with his mouth, felt his lover's tongue wanting him.

Orlando decided he could get used to that dog after all.

New from the #1 bestselling author of *Communion*—
a novel of psychological terror and demonic possession. . . .
"A triumph."—Peter Straub

UNHOLY
FIRE
Whitley Strieber

Father John Rafferty is a dedicated priest with only one
temptation—the beautiful young woman he has been coun-
seling, and who is found brutally murdered in his Green-
wich Village church. He is forced to face his greatest test
of faith when the NYPD uncovers her sexually twisted
hidden life, and the church becomes the site for increas-
ingly violent acts. Father Rafferty knows he must overcome his personal horror to unmask a murderer who
wears an angel's face. This chilling novel will hold you in
thrall as it explores the powerful forces of evil lurking
where we least expect them. "Gyrates with evil energy
. . . fascinating church intrigue."—*Kirkus Reviews*

There's an epidemic with 27 million victims. And no visible symptoms.

It's an epidemic of people who can't read.

Believe it or not, 27 million Americans are functionally illiterate, about one adult in five.

The solution to this problem is you... when you join the fight against illiteracy. So call the Coalition for Literacy at toll-free 1-800-228-8813 and volunteer.

Volunteer Against Illiteracy. The only degree you need is a degree of caring.